Toaru Majutsu no
Index Light Novel
es

A Certain Magical Index

14

KAZUMA KAMACHI

ILLUSTRATION BY
KIYOTAKA HAIMURA

"I was just trying to shut these morons up!!"

Kamijou's classmate **Seiri Fukiyose**

"...D-don't tell me you were part of this ridiculous argument, too..."

Math teacher at Kamijou's school **Suama Oyafune**

"In conclusion, lolis look good in anything, so obviously, a bunny girl loli would still be the best, meeeow!!"

Kamijou's classmate **Motoharu Tsuchimikado**

"I knew it! This isn't even *about* bunny girls to you!!"

Level Zero Academy City High School student **Touma Kamijou**

"…What are you hoping to gain?"

Roman Orthodox disciple
also known as the Mardi Gras
Lidvia Lorenzetti

"Why don't you bring in those puritanical torture devices you're so proud of? Then I'll show you the depths of my faith, you inexperienced whelp."

Roman Orthodox bishop
Biagio Busoni

" ..... "

Former Roman Orthodox sister **Agnes Sanctis**

"Do not belittle
Necessarius."

English Puritan
sorcerer from
Necessarius
Stiyl Magnus

"......?"

Amakusa-
Style
Crossist
Church
follower
Itsuwa

"My turn on the stage has come
at last. For you see, God's Right Seat
cannot use the normal sorcery of
humans. I'd very much appreciate it if
you would let me have a little fun."

Member of the Roman Orthodox Church's
God's Right Seat **Terra of the Left**

contents

A Certain Magical Index

VOLUME 14

KAZUMA KAMACHI

ILLUSTRATION BY: KIYOTAKA HAIMURA

NEW YORK

A CERTAIN MAGICAL INDEX, Volume 14
KAZUMA KAMACHI

Translation by Andrew Prowse
Cover art by Kiyotaka Haimura

TOARU MAJYUTSU NO INDEX
©KAZUMA KAMACHI 2007
All rights reserved.
Edited by ASCII MEDIA WORKS
First published in Japan in 2007 by KADOKAWA CORPORATION, Tokyo.
English translation rights arranged with KADOKAWA CORPORATION, Tokyo, through Tuttle-Mori Agency, Inc., Tokyo.

English translation © 2018 by Yen Press, LLC

Yen On
1290 Avenue of the Americas
New York, NY 10104

Visit us at yenpress.com
facebook.com/yenpress
twitter.com/yenpress
yenpress.tumblr.com
instagram.com/yenpress

First Yen On Edition: February 2018

Yen On is an imprint of Yen Press, LLC.
The Yen On name and logo are trademarks of Yen Press, LLC.

The publisher is not responsible for websites (or their content) that are not owned by the publisher.

Library of Congress Cataloging-in-Publication Data

Names: Kamachi, Kazuma, author. | Haimura, Kiyotaka, 1973– illustrator. | Prowse, Andrew (Andrew R.), translator. | Hinton, Yoshito, translator.
Title: A certain magical index / Kazuma Kamachi ; illustration by Kiyotaka Haimura.
Other titles: To aru majyutsu no kinsho mokuroku. (Light novel). English
Description: First Yen On edition. | New York : Yen On, 2014–
Identifiers: LCCN 2014031047 (print) | ISBN 9780316339124 (v. 1 : pbk.) |
    ISBN 9780316259422 (v. 2 : pbk.) | ISBN 9780316340540 (v. 3 : pbk.) |
    ISBN 9780316340564 (v. 4 : pbk.) | ISBN 9780316340595 (v. 5 : pbk.) |
    ISBN 9780316340601 (v. 6 : pbk.) | ISBN 9780316272230 (v. 7 : pbk.) |
    ISBN 9780316359924 (v. 8 : pbk.) | ISBN 9780316359962 (v. 9 : pbk.) |
    ISBN 9780316359986 (v. 10: pbk.) | ISBN 9780316360005 (v. 11: pbk.) |
    ISBN 9780316360029 (v. 12: pbk.) | ISBN 9780316442671 (v. 13: pbk.) |
    ISBN 9780316442701 (v. 14: pbk.)
Subjects: | CYAC: Magic—Fiction. | Ability—Fiction. | Nuns—Fiction. | Japan—Fiction. | Science fiction. | BISAC: FICTION / Fantasy / General. | FICTION / Science Fiction / Adventure.
Classification: LCC PZ7.1.K215 Ce 2014 | DDC [Fic]—dc23
LC record available at https://lccn.loc.gov/2014031047

ISBNs: 978-0-316-44270-1 (paperback)
       978-0-316-44271-8 (ebook)

1 3 5 7 9 10 8 6 4 2

LSC-C

Printed in the United States of America

PROLOGUE

A Church Too Dark

Bread_and_Wine.

Terra of the Left.

He was in St. Peter's Square in the Vatican. It was an oval-shaped park about 240 meters wide with a public fountain a short distance away from its center. Terra sat on the edge of that flowing creation, quietly looking up at the stars overhead.

With few man-made lights in the square, his face wasn't visible. Only the gentle darkness enveloped his silhouette, operating as a kind of veil.

There came a small splash.

It wasn't from the fountain.

In Terra's right hand was a bottle filled with cheap red wine. He didn't have a drinking glass to accompany it; each time he brought the bottle to his lips, the alcohol contained within made a splashing ripple.

Nonetheless, there was no air of inebriation to him.

If it had been daytime and his face visible, all who saw him would think to themselves, *What awful wine that man drinks*. He wore the expression of someone working overtime.

"Are you drinking again, Terra?"

He heard a low, masculine voice. He turned his head back to look that way, remaining seated on the fountain's edge. It was another member of God's Right Seat—Acqua of the Back. The man wore mainly blue clothing, which resembled a golfing outfit.

Next to him was an old man wrapped in magnificent ceremonial robes.

The Roman Orthodox pope.

He was supposedly the most powerful person in the Vatican, but the two God's Right Seat members obscured the man's presence to a mysterious degree.

Terra wiped the red liquid dripping from the corner of his lips with an arm and said, "I am technically replenishing myself, you know. With the blood of God."

"Bread and wine," said Acqua. "Just like Mass."

"My Raphael, the healing of God, signifies earth. The land's fruits and blessings are the quickest way to replenish my strength."

He thought he'd answered seriously, but Acqua and the pope both sighed. Each let their eyes drop to Terra's feet.

Around them were several empty bottles.

After seeing the label on one, Acqua shook his head. "Cheap wine," he said. "You can't find wine this cheap even in stores trying to rip off tourists. You could have gotten a slightly better brand if you'd said you were with God's Right Seat."

"Please stop it," said Terra good-naturedly. "I don't understand the intricacies of wine. It's only a tool for a ritual, after all. If I asked for more, I'd be insulting *real* alcoholics."

After hearing the pair's exchange, the pope interjected, "...As a mentor to the faithful, though, I would prefer that you abstain from gaudier drink."

"Oh. Well, I didn't expect you to be criticizing *me*." Terra laughed in a low voice. "Wine is only necessary for this ritual. But you, Acqua, don't need any such thing—yet you seem to know quite a bit about tastes and brands."

The pope glared at Acqua, who winced slightly. Unlike the other members, he didn't make light of the pope, for some reason. "A carry-over from my days as a mercenary," the man explained. "One of the battlefield's necessities."

"Ha-ha, well, you are a hoodlum, Acqua," laughed Terra. "A bad boy, unlike the rest of us pious believers."

The pope grimaced at this casual recommendation of himself. Being lumped together with the man was, perhaps, not something he appreciated.

As if to offset this, the pope took a moment to view the square that could hold three hundred thousand people. "Still...," he said in the quiet of the night. "Two of God's Right Seat and even the pope of Roman Orthodoxy outdoors without actual protection...Should we not hold these meetings inside? If security saw us now, they might start foaming at the mouth."

"I think it's fine, don't you? The Croce di Pietro is still in effect," said Terra, taking a sip of wine and looking up at the night sky. *"And just look at how disgusting the sky here is.* There are so many barriers colliding and competing that it looks like the aurora up there. It would be hard to magically snipe someone through all that."

All spells, not just barriers, could be countered and reverse engineered if you solved their formulas. The library of grimoires that Puritanism was so proud about, the Index of Forbidden Books, was the culmination of that idea.

However, the layered barriers protecting the entire nation were intertwined by the Crossist "meanings" held by over 90 percent of the Vatican's buildings, forming a complex web. Analysis with the Index of Forbidden Books wasn't an option—even the nation's highest authority, the pope, could no longer grasp the entirety of it.

One could spend a long time breaking an intricate cipher, but if the password's pattern changed every second, any old solutions would lose meaning. Not only did the keyhole change shape; the number of keyholes changed, too, making it impossible to create a duplicate key.

Despite the Roman Orthodox Church—the pope first and foremost—no longer having anyone who could enact clear controls over the barriers layered around the Vatican, the shield still brushed off every analysis spell that came knocking.

"In any case," began Terra.

He put the now-empty wine bottle on the fountain's edge. That was the last of the cheap booze he'd brought into the sanctuary.

With slow motions, he rose to his feet, straightened his back a little, and said, "Now that I'm done replenishing the blood of God, I suppose I should be on my way."

Acqua's eyebrows moved slightly. "You're using *it*, then?"

Terra's lips opened thinly, and he laughed. He could tell from Acqua's tone of voice that feelings of bitterness swirled inside the man. "You disapprove of using civilians, Acqua?"

"...Bloody battles are better left to the soldiers who thrive on it."

"Ha-ha," laughed Terra pleasantly. "A real *noble* viewpoint. Unfortunately..." He paused. "The Church's greatest weapon is its numbers. The figure *two billion* is a big strong point. Begrudging the fact is less natural. Academy City only has 2.3 million in all. Different literally by orders of magnitude."

"War decided by the quantity of people and goods?" said Acqua. "Barbaric. I feel as though I'm peering into a war of ancient times."

"The simplest solutions truly haven't changed at all since back then," countered Terra, looking up at the sky through the canopy of barriers. Despite having practically drowned himself in wine, his gait didn't waver in the slightest. "We of God's Right Seat may be imperfect, but we lead the people with the mystery of those imperfections."

He spread his hands to the side, stood on one foot, then swiveled around to Acqua.

"Why not let the scared lambs seek guidance where they will? By my shepherd's hands...just like the children who vanished after the piper."

CHAPTER 1

The Speed of Too Soon a Change

In_a_Long-Distance_Country.

1

Academy City's School District 3 had several international exhi-bition halls, and it was connected to School District 23, the city's ocean-facing front door, by a direct railroad line. The former pos-sessed many facilities for visitors from abroad, like hotels (all of the highest grade in the city), while the latter held all the airports. The distance and distinction between the amenities of the two was to curb flight noise around the city's upscale lodging.

The city hosted many of its events in District 3. Some were motor shows collecting the very best in self-driving technology, while oth-ers were robotics expositions featuring the fruits of mechanical engi-neering. These exhibitions weren't purely for fun projects—mostly, they were for promoting the city's cutting-edge tech. City officials would present technology approved by the General Board to be of the proper standard to put to use outside the city, select the trade offers from the countless outside corporations that were most bene-ficial (not *search*—for Academy City, it was always *select*), and amass huge amounts of funding.

Another of those such shows was going on today.

On display were, among other things, unmanned attack helicopters, the latest in exoskeletal powered suit apparatuses, and even high-output optical weapons that could aid in aerial bombing.

Even the event's name was the Interceptor Weaponry Show, showing how absurdly dangerous everything was.

"Pfhaaa…"

Someone let out a deep breath—a girl in the domed exhibition hall's corner with a powered suit attached to her torso, making the act look oddly humorous.

"It's so hot…," grumbled Yomikawa, her helmet tucked under her arm. "Why are these powered suit demonstrations so exhausting?"

Next to her, a woman in work clothes shot her a glance. She was a member of the powered suit development team, looking as out of place in her outfit as a small child in a tuxedo; she was used to a white lab coat.

"Don't worry, it's not just you," she said. "There's a lot of hot air floating around the hall."

A laptop rested on the engineer's knees. There was a thin card reminiscent of a cell phone inserted in its side. Its screen displayed technical data for their exoskeletons.

"Look, that doesn't make me any happier, 'kay?"

"I didn't say it to make you happy."

"Still, I wonder why there's so many gosh-darn *people* here," Yomikawa went on. "An interceptor weaponry show on a weekday is pretty hard-core, y'know? Doesn't this hall look like it's over capacity?"

"Actually, it's press day, so there aren't many here. Tomorrow it'll be open to everyone. It'll look like hell."

"Look, that doesn't make me any happier, 'kay?"

"I didn't say it to make you happy."

Terribly discouraged by her engineer, Yomikawa placed the helmet under her arm on the floor with a clatter. The helmet was almost fifty centimeters across. It had looked like she'd been wearing one of the oil-drum-shaped city-patrolling robots on her head. The rest of the powered suit resembled thick plate armor, making the whole thing look pretty top-heavy.

"So hot. You know what, I'm just gonna take off the rest...," she said, wriggling her neck out, then continuing to crawl out of the suit. Underneath the armor, she wore black clothing, like the kind special forces used.

Yomikawa sat down with her back against the motionless mech suit and started futilely fanning herself with a hand. "Jeez, these really aren't made for wearing in combat suits, eh? Wonder if there's a more breathable exoskel-exclusive outfit lying around."

"I guess you should have gone along with the planning head's idea. Take off the suit, and *bam!* a knockout bikini. It'd get a lot of applause from the press. They'd be ecstatic."

As far as Yomikawa could tell from the monotone, the engineer didn't care one bit about her problem. She used a towel to wipe off the beads of sweat sticking to her face. "That guy gets way too into it whenever we start talking about promotional models."

"It's probably his hobby, sadly."

"You couldn't find a more boorish woman in all Japan than me. I could never pretend to be a booth babe. How on earth did I end up in his sights?"

"I guess Anti-Skill has it pretty rough, huh? They make you do odd jobs like you're the SDF or something."

"If we get odd jobs, it means there's nothing else to do and the world's at peace. Still..." Yomikawa stopped and looked around.

Booths all over were displaying a myriad of tools for killing people. The usual tinge of "capturing berserk espers while doing the least damage possible" had been stashed in a corner. Instead, one could see nothing but super-powerful, highly lethal weapons—the sort that would penetrate a tank if a person tried to hide behind it, and then them, too.

The booth organizers had certainly changed course quickly. *And there's only one reason I can think of...*

Yomikawa stole a glance at the laptop the engineer was using. Along with a diagram of the powered suit she'd just been demonstrating was a small window showing a television feed. It was a news program, with a reporter reading from a manuscript.

"Early this morning local time, large-scale religious protests have broken out in the industrial city of Toulouse in southern France," said the newscaster. *"People have flooded onto a road several kilometers long that follows the Garonne River, which runs through the center of the city, and they continue to severely affect infrastructure networks like transportation."*

The program showed a recorded video of a pitch-black city lit brightly by torch flame, with massive crowds of people marching along. Some of the men and women carried banners with French vilification written on them, while other young people were setting fire to Academy City signboards and holding them aloft.

Technically, they were only protesting—these weren't uncontrolled riots. Still, the sight of thousands parading through the streets with their anger on full display intimidated Yomikawa enough to give her a chill.

"In Dortmund, in central Germany, a bulldozer thought to be stolen has rammed into a Roman Orthodox church, severely wounding nine priests inside. Authorities believe it's retribution for the recent string of protests, but nobody has claimed responsibility yet. With worries of the conflict between the Roman Orthodox Church and Academy City escalating in the future on the rise…"

She'd seen it already, but she couldn't shake the bitter feeling. Like a tiny ember spreading to a dry heap of straw, the world had changed a lot these past few days. With the Roman Orthodox Church's simultaneous worldwide demonstrations and certain people's overreactions to them, the conflict was accelerating by the second.

And now, Academy City was throwing an interceptor weaponry exhibition as though in response. At a glance, one could take it to be the General Board officially announcing that the city would not yield to the protests.

But this…was all executed too well for that, she thought.

Weapons development wasn't like building plastic models. One had to submit an application for development, go back and forth with budget proposals, carefully discuss it, design prototypes, do hundreds if not *thousands* of simulations with what they built, hammer out the numbers they were looking for, and only then would they have a "product" to display.

The string of demonstrations had worsened just these past few days. Weapons development needed years of work. They couldn't possibly keep up. Which meant...

Academy City was already prepared for this, she thought. *They foresaw this happening to the world, and instead of stopping it before it started, they plotted to have control of things after the fact, didn't they? Shit.* It made her want to spit.

Maybe Academy City wouldn't be the one to pull the trigger on a war, but it was clearly trying to profit from the idea.

The engineer, owner of the laptop, used her sleeve to wipe the sweat from her brow and reluctantly looked over at the news screen. "Every channel's the same thing. Times like these make me wish I had a contract for variety show channels or something."

"...What do you think?"

"Hmm." The weapons research scientist paused briefly. "I don't like having more work. Unpaid overtime is even worse."

"This expo is totally different from usual, isn't it?"

"Well, the head of planning was really into it. Saying things about overturning the foul stereotypes of the defense industry and thus opening up new markets. Crazy stuff, if you ask me. This whole place is specifically for developing weapons. He looked delirious from the heat, so I hit him with an ice cube."

"The technology they're showing off clearly isn't to sell to outside companies. Which basically makes this a military exercise...Showing our 'enemies' only the destructive power of a swarm of unknown weaponry, using intimidation to play the diplomacy card—that's all we're doing."

"I suppose. They are quite destructive. The head of planning lost a few screws because of it, though, and he started blurting out even more nonsense."

"They might be making deals on these products, but it's not like we're shipping the ones on display," said Yomikawa. "It's like taking the full-auto function out of rifles and lining them up in your storefront. We're just selling them stuff three or four generations worse…And even those are just barely reproducible by the technology outside Academy City." Yomikawa looked at a group of men in business suits talking to one another right next to a nearby platform. "Plus, we're talking about buying and selling licenses, but the only facilities in *any* country that can manufacture the core components of these weapons are already aligned with this city. Meaning we can tell exactly how many are produced and where they're deployed to. Jeez, why does Academy City go so far to get money?"

"With enough capital, it can mass-produce silly weapons," said the engineer. "The head of planning is apparently trying to send a giant humanoid robot into space next. And I bet the pilot candidate will be a teenage boy, too."

"…You really have no enthusiasm for this, huh?"

"Not in the slightest."

2

Though Aiho Yomikawa had no way of knowing, a certain boy *was* at the middle of this great conflict.

Touma Kamijou.

Other than his power, Imagine Breaker, he was supposed to be a totally normal high school student. But if what God's Right Seat had said was right, he was now an enemy of two billion people. Thinking back on the incidents he'd been wrapped up in these last few months and how gradually they'd all been resolved, though, it seemed reasonable.

And so, this boy Touma Kamijou, relatively central to the conflict…

"—Now, I want you to tell me why you did something like this."

…was being lectured harshly by a tall female teacher in the faculty room.

To be more precise, he wasn't the only one being lectured. Blue

Hair and Motoharu Tsuchimikado were right there with him, hanging their heads. Seiri Fukiyose was behind them, too, looking frustrated, wondering why she'd been called here.

The faculty room was filled with haphazardly placed office desks made of steel. Many teachers were around, probably because it was lunchtime. They were doing all sorts of things, like eating meals, grading tests, and riding electric wooden horses to lower their body weight.

Their teacher, Suama Oyafune, wasn't eating a meal, nor grading tests, nor riding an electric wooden horse to control her body weight. Instead, she was sitting on a cheap-looking swivel chair, her legs crossed and clad in beige stockings, combing her hard, needlelike hair up with a hand, and glaring at the students out of brand-name inverted triangular glasses that must have been expensive.

"I'll ask again. Explain to me why you thought it would be all right to get into a huge brawl in the school building and have a lively clash of burning souls with your fists as weapons."

Silence.

A TV on the room's wall was broadcasting the news. *"Because of repeated demonstration marches and protests, Italian soccer leagues have determined their stadiums unsafe and suspended their morning games."*

"You can't explain it?" she demanded. This irritable teacher who always wore brand-name clothing and accessories was famous at Kamijou's school for being particularly strict with "disciplining." She was in charge of a different class, so they really hadn't talked to her much, but today she'd been the one to catch them.

Their class's homeroom teacher was Komoe Tsukuyomi, but even she couldn't keep an eye on the classroom during lunch break. Suama Oyafune had happened to walk by during their fight, then captured them and dragged them off to the faculty room by the proverbial ear.

"I mean...," said Kamijou, steeling himself and looking straight at the teacher, eyes glinting. "Come on! Blue Hair and I were arguing about whether red or black bunny girls were better, and then suddenly

Tsuchimikado comes in and calls us idiots and says, *White ones are obviously best*, and that doesn't even make any sense!"

Clatter-clatter! Suama and her chair flipped over.

The volume of Kamijou's voice was one thing, but the opinion must have been a little too stimulating for a teacher wearing inverted equilaterals.

The math teacher looked away from the three idiots to Seiri Fukiyose, who was standing behind them.

"...D-don't tell me you were part of this ridiculous argument, too..."

"I was just trying to shut these morons up!!" shouted Fukiyose in reply, blood vessels appearing near her temples. "Why did I get dragged here, too?!"

Still, when Oyafune had stepped into their classroom, Fukiyose had Tsuchimikado in a headlock, had already kicked Blue Hair to the floor, and was in the process of giving Touma Kamijou a forehead slam. She was doubtlessly number one, the boss of the kids.

Meanwhile, Tsuchimikado, wearing his blue sunglasses, shook his head from side to side. "Flat-chested white bunnies for the win, meowsa."

Blue Hair couldn't stay silent about that. "S-stop making everything flat, you asshole!! Besides, you're not even into bunny girls! You'd take anything as long as it was a loli!!"

"But it's the truth, nya, Blue Hair. When faced with such a powerful loli, any tiny, insignificant clothing attributes like bunny suits or gymnastic leotards or school swimsuits mean nothing. In conclusion, lolis look good in anything, so obviously, a bunny girl loli would still be the best, meeeow!!"

"Say that again!!" cried Kamijou. "I knew it! This isn't even *about* bunny girls to you!!"

As the three idiots rolled up their sleeves and got ready for round two, the triangle glasses–wearing, suit-clad lady professor Suama Oyafune, who was still overturned with her chair, took out a whistle and blew.

Pfweeeee!! came the whistle's shrill command as the gorilla-like civic guidance teacher, Mr. Saigo, stood up at the back of the faculty room and lumbered over.

3

In the end, they were all ordered to do some weeding behind the gymnasium after school.

With little exposure to the sun, the area was damp, with weeds energetically overtaking the place. Just looking at how big the green surface was made Kamijou lose the will to work, and the thought *Why bother cleaning if nobody comes back here?* permeated the air from every mind.

However, something else was really responsible for draining his enthusiasm.

"Tsu-Tsuchimikado, Blue Hair, I'll get you back for this vanishing act..."

Right now, out of the four ordered to weed, only Kamijou and Fukiyose were here.

Abandoned and alone, Kamijou's shoulders drooped as he stared at the vast area behind the gym. On the other side of that thin wall, he could hear high-spirited voices he just knew were from the volleyball or basketball club as they enjoyed their after-school time to the fullest. It made the heavy mental chains of this unproductive weeding all the heavier.

Still, muttering under his breath about his nemeses disappearing wouldn't make the weeds go away. Kamijou picked up a pair of work gloves from a wheelbarrow he'd brought over to carry the weeds to the garbage area, stating, "We're not gonna be done weeding by the time they kick us out for the night anyway. Let's just take it easy until then."

He continued under his breath, "It'd be over a lot faster if we could get a pyrokinetic over here, too."

Fukiyose wasn't happy about being sucked into this, either, but she was pulling out the weeds more efficiently than her grumbling partner.

Five minutes later, having grown bored, Kamijou once more

spoke to the girl squatting down a short distance away. "By the way, Fukiyose..."

"What is it?" She must have been bored, too, because it didn't take any coaxing to get her to respond.

Kamijou started moving his hands again. "Weren't they talking about suspending midterms in October? But you're still using all your free time to study for them by yourself. How come?"

"What, that?" she asked curtly. "If we don't have midterms, that means our second semester grades are gonna be based only on our finals. And the finals will probably be at least twice as big. That's even more reason not to let up, isn't it?"

"..."

"And I'm not letting you see my notes."

Kamijou had been on cloud nine, thinking *No more midterms, whoopee!* but Fukiyose delivered the finishing blow with no concern.

The unexpected hit put Kamijou into coward mode. "H-hmph. School studies aren't everything, you know!"

"You make it sound like studying is all I can do."

"...You can do something else?"

"Yes!!" shouted Fukiyose from her stomach. "I may not look like it, but I can throw a forkball. Not that I have any real interest in baseball!!"

"Really," said Kamijou slowly. "Not from online classes or some kind of forkball health exercise, I bet."

"It...It doesn't matter how I learned it. All that matters is if I can pitch one or not! Don't give me that suspicious look—I'll prove it to you!!"

"Yeah, yeah. But we don't have a ball." Kamijou sighed.

Fukiyose took a ball the size of her fist out of her skirt pocket. "You can never be too prepared!!"

"...Um, that ball has something written on it. 'Squeeze this ball one hundred times a day to facilitate alpha waves...'"

Kamijou gaped, but the girl didn't care. She actually seemed pretty motivated and started digging at the ground a little with one foot.

Kamijou had no catcher's mitt for the ball, so instead, he put on several pairs of work gloves. He walked away with no small degree of reluctance, then squatted and did his best impression of a catcher's pose.

When he spoke, his words were monotone, like one big, long sigh. "Go ahead, Fukiyose."

"All right, Kamijou. Don't be too impressed by my amazing one hundred and fifty kilometers per hour pitch!!"

"A one hundred and fifty kilometers per hour forkball?!" he cried in a fluster. "I'm already impressed by that amazing bluff!!"

Fukiyose, really getting into it now, gripped the white ball, slowly turned, and held it overhead.

It was just a windup, but Kamijou suddenly shouted, "S-stop, stop, Fukiyose!!"

"What do you want?!" she shouted back unsteadily, stopped midway through her pitching form.

But Kamijou had hesitated to give it to her straight, so he skipped the important parts and said, "*Skirt!!*"

"…?"

Fukiyose frowned, searching for the meaning in his gaze. She looked around her waist area, discovering there that holding up her knee had flipped up her skirt and revealed her cutely patterned underwear…

…before launching an overpowering fastball.

Kamijou missed the timing, and the soft rubber ball slammed into his belly with a hard, violent *splat!!*

As Kamijou writhed in agony, he spoke, voice trembling. "…Th-that wasn't a forkball. You just threw it as hard as you freaking could…"

"That one didn't count!!" shouted Fukiyose, giving a quite masculine excuse, as she caught the ball from Kamijou. "Jeez. This time I'll throw a forkball. It'll drop pretty quick, so put your mitt lower."

Saying something or other, Fukiyose began to go through the pitching motion, but since Kamijou had pointed out her skirt a moment ago, her leg movements ended up rather stiff.

Her balance was a bit wobbly because of that, but the pitch she threw had an astounding amount of force behind it. With a *splat!!*

the ball struck the layers of work gloves he wore. It wasn't even a hardball, just a toy, but it still stung his palm. Plus, she hadn't thrown it underhanded like a softball player but overhanded like a pro baseball pitcher, and that sealed the deal.

Kamijou squeezed the ball a little. "Did that...drop?"

"Yes, it did!! Weren't you watching? Couldn't you tell it dropped right before it got to the batter?!"

"Huh? It just looked like you threw it normally."

"K-Kamijou!! You weren't standing where the batter should be, so you wouldn't know!! If you actually swung a bat, you would have realized how sharp my forkball is!!"

"Oh. Well, now you've said it, Fukiyose." Kamijou smirked and took a small plastic-handled broom about fifty centimeters long from a few dustpan sets he'd brought just in case. "That sounded a lot like a challenge to me."

Gripping the handle vaguely like a baseball bat, he rolled his hands on his wrists to gauge the timing of his swing.

Meanwhile, Fukiyose, for her part, having caught the ball Kamijou tossed back, gave a fearless grin. "Trying to beat Major League Fukiyose's pitch, are you? You're pretty funny—for a monkey."

"I'll knock this one out."

"I'll show you—the drop of a true forkball and the humiliation of defeeeat!!"

"Right out of the paaaaaaaaaaaark!!"

A baseball thrown.

The sound of air parting.

If he waited to see if it really dropped, he'd be far too late on the swing.

Unable to assess Fukiyose's true intent and ability, he moved to answer her challenge.

Power and tension coursed through his body.

He judged the timing, exhaled slightly, set his feet, turned his hips with his arms, swung the broom in both hands as hard as he could...

And...

4

Suama Oyafune, clad in a suit, inverted triangle glasses, and even stockings—all brand-name—understood that beautiful women had an advantage.

Of course, she only knew that because she'd been relegated to *constantly having disadvantages in the past.*

Anybody, no matter what they looked like, could become beautiful to some extent. Suama's theory went like this: Even if "high level" or "mid-high level" was aiming too high, "high middle" was perfectly doable. And if she got up to that "high middle" level, she'd begin to see the benefits here and there.

Beautiful people had an advantage.

Her students would listen to what she was saying in class, her fellow teachers wouldn't look down on her, and some would even give her their seats in the cafeteria. All of these advantages came from spending an hour in the bath every day, putting on face lotion before bed, eating a proper breakfast every morning, managing her weight so it wouldn't affect her skin, dedicating over an hour to putting on makeup before leaving, and freely using magazines and the Internet to shop around for Western-style clothes—a boon gained from keeping herself polished, both on the outside and the inside.

For Suama Oyafune, her makeup starting to fall off after school let out—especially if sweat was making her drawn-on eyebrows run—was a major source of anxiety. Still, beauty was defined by one's attitude and aura, too. If she was too obviously worried about her makeup, she would gain less of the benefits of being beautiful, so checking mirrors over and over and going back and forth to the powder room wouldn't be good.

...

Suama slowly looked around.

She was in the faculty room. At this hour, most teachers had gone to advise their clubs, so it was thinned out. If nobody was around, maybe she'd secretly check her eyebrows...

"Phew~! Making handouts sure is hard work!"

In a seat relatively close to her was a teacher who looked like an elementary school student, hectically working.

Komoe Tsukuyomi.

The stack of papers clearly exceeded what any one person could be expected to handle. This tiny teacher was known for creating the most effective teaching materials based off precise data on each individual student, but she must have been undertaking other teachers' work, too.

Right now, with the city's peacekeeping Anti-Skill being rounded up in great numbers, they didn't have time to make every single thing for their classes. Other non-Anti-Skill teachers would have to help them out.

Even Suama had handouts and such to make for other teachers, but the woman couldn't help but be more interested in Komoe Tsukuyomi's "minimalism."

"...What kind of health routines do you need to keep such young and lustrous skin? Actually, mathematically speaking, those values are impossible."

"??? What is? I'm pretty good at math, so I can help you."

One hundred and thirty-five centimeters quickly came pattering up to her after hearing her greatly perplexed voice. Suama admitted there were several things she could learn from the tiny woman as a teacher, but was anyone *sure* she wasn't actually in elementary school?

Komoe Tsukuyomi came over and took the papers on Suama's desk without asking, then went over them one by one, nodding to herself. "By the way, Ms. Oyafune, did my students cause you trouble? I apologize for that."

"No, not at all."

"Oh yes. As his teacher, I would like to take Kami and the others to task as well. Do you know where they are? They left right after homeroom. Have they gone home already?"

"Oh no," said Suama in a louder voice, reflexively looking at the clock hanging on the wall.

It was almost six o'clock.

It had been *hours* since she'd told them to weed.

"Ack…I'm sorry, Ms. Komoe, I'll go get them right now!!"

"Well, okay. But where are they?"

The relaxed senior teacher's words came at her back; Suama had already burst out of the faculty room. Club activities were winding down, too, and nobody who didn't belong to an after-school club could be seen. The hallways were dim and mostly empty, so as she walked toward the faculty entrance, she quickly began to feel how much time had actually passed.

Well, delinquents who cause fights at school shouldn't have that much patience. They've probably gone home already without doing any of the weeding.

Still, she'd meant to check on them after about half an hour, then scold them a little and make them go home, so she couldn't help but feel reluctant now. It had been a rash punishment, so she also couldn't easily apologize to the students now.

Meanwhile, after reaching the faculty entrance and changing into her relatively high-class pumps, she hurried behind the gymnasium.

And there, the inverted triangle glasses–wearing female math teacher saw…

5

"Come on, come on!! Thirteen wins, nine losses—that forkball of yours is nothing!!" challenged Kamijou, gripping his short broom with both hands and waggling it at Fukiyose.

"Be quiet!! Nine losses, and you're still running your mouth… Besides, if we were using a real hardball, it would spin a lot better!!"

After introducing a rule where each loss equated to five minutes of full-power weeding, the match between Kamijou and Fukiyose had gotten seriously heated. Their high school souls burned with such ferocity that it would make one forget that if they just took it easy and did the work together, it would have been much easier.

Unlike Kamijou, who was quite happily swinging the bat, Fukiyose was breathing heavily as she kept a firm grasp on the baseball, her shoulders moving up and down. She checked the time on her cell phone. "Besides, there's still thirty minutes until schools close... That's enough time to turn it around!!"

"By the way, are your pitches dropping like they're supposed to?"

"I keep telling you they are! They're forking great!! Why can't you tell that they're dropping suddenly right before getting to home plate?!"

"Really? I feel like they're just slowing down and falling like anything else would..."

"Get a closer looooooooooook!!"

Fukiyose, roaring with all her might, lobbed the ball.

Whhhrrrrrr!! In response to the approaching baseball, Kamijou wound up for a full swing.

A forkball...

But then his body reacted unconsciously to Fukiyose's words, causing him to adjust the short broom's course down a little.

Once again, however, the ball didn't curve much at all.

A normal straight pitch flew at him.

"You...You can't do it after all!!"

He quickly tried to bring the bat back on track, but he was too late. Nevertheless, he felt the ball's edge nick the broomstick.

"Gwoooohhhhhhhhhhh!!" bellowed Kamijou even as he felt the hitting sensation fade.

After taking a chip out of the broomstick, the baseball curved slightly upward and continued to fly behind him.

Shit, I missed?!

Fouls were a concept that didn't exist for this contest. If Kamijou hit the ball in front of him, he won, but otherwise, Fukiyose won. They made vague judgments to decide whether her pitches were strikes or balls.

Plus—and this was the really annoying part—whoever lost had to go get the ball. The loser already had to do five minutes of full-power weeding as punishment. Having to chase down faraway balls was a huge pain.

So he stood there for a second in his pose, broomstick still out to the side, instantly starting calculations in his head. *Gah. That's thirteen wins and nine losses. No, wait, ten losses. Maybe I'll filibuster her, walk real slowly to go get it...*

Smack.

Then he heard an odd noise from right behind him.

"...?"

He didn't understand, but Fukiyose, who was facing him, had a shocked expression and was standing stock-still. He could practically hear the blood in her face retreating.

??? Is there something behind me?

When Kamijou turned around...

...he saw grass and dirt stuck to inverted triangle–shaped glasses...

...and, wearing them, the teacher Suama Oyafune, clearly having taken the ball to the face.

The baseball would have hit her in the stomach if not for Kamijou's swing glancing off it and changing its course—right into her face.

"..."

Suama Oyafune was taking slow, deep breaths, but she was obviously trembling.

*Ahhh, aaahhhhhhh...*By the time Kamijou started shaking, it was too late.

Suama Oyafune plunged toward him and swung a clenched fist just as Kamijou, unaware, went down on his hands and knees in prostration, coincidentally dodging her knuckles, and now, the math teacher's anger at the ball and at her own missed attack compounding each other, she drove the sharp heel of her pump into his back.

6

Suama Oyafune hastened back to the faculty room.

Ms. Komoe was absent; she must have gone somewhere.

Technically, she'd already gotten the grass and dirt off her face with a handkerchief, but still...

Waaah!! Dirt, dirt, dirt!! It's stuck to my face, I just know it! And maybe my penciled eyebrows are coming off because I accidentally wiped them!! What to do, what do I do, aghhh?!!

Her panic was so pronounced a blind person could have seen it. She made sure nobody was around before forgetting about going to the powder room and taking out a hand mirror to check her face right then and there.

For now, her eyebrows were fine.

But that wasn't enough to relieve Suama Oyafune.

Beautiful women had advantages. If she wasn't beautiful, she would be disadvantaged. That was how life worked.

Okay, so my clothes—dirty. Over here, too. And over here?! My hair's a mess, I'm sweating, my stockings are running from walking so fast, where do I even start?!

For now, she took her suit jacket off, brushed off the flecks of dirt that made it to her white blouse. But some clung stubbornly, so she took the blouse off and shook it out.

Then she removed her running beige stockings so she could change into the spare pair she had in her purse. Due to the way she moved, her tight skirt turned all the way up during that, but she didn't have time to worry about it. She had to go back to being the perfect, beautiful teacher as soon as she could.

But then…

…the faculty room door started clattering.

Suama froze, one leg raised to put through her stocking.

"Wait…I…wait!!" she said immediately.

"Huh? For what?"

She knew he'd heard her, and yet the door clattered open anyway.

It was Touma Kamijou.

And Suama Oyafune, her blouse open in the front and her black underwear visible, her tight skirt flipped up so she could put on her stockings, stayed absolutely still.

"Ky—"

She checked herself just before screaming.

Instead, she reached for a nearby desk and grabbed a fifty-centimeter super-large triangle ruler with a magnet for using on blackboards in class. Then she hurled it with all her might at the faculty room entrance.

Kamijou quickly slammed the door shut, and the triangle's tip stabbed the doorframe like a shuriken. The lodged ruler wobbled back and forth.

A shout echoed into the room from the hallway. "Ooowwahh-hhh!! That could have killed me!!"

"Explain to me right now why you came in after I told you to wait!!"

For the moment, she pulled the stockings the rest of the way up, closed the front of her blouse, put her arms through the suit jacket she'd hung over the back of her chair, and hurriedly started for the hallway when...

Brk.

This time, she heard a strange noise from near her thighs.

"..."

She'd just unsealed these stockings two minutes ago. *Are they running already?* thought Suama, thoughtlessly checking her thighs.

"U-um, excuse me..."

As if he'd timed it that way, Touma Kamijou nervously opened the faculty room door once again.

To see Suama Oyafune, her legs in an O shape, her tight skirt up, bent over and looking around her crotch area.

Beauty aside—the scene did enough damage to her very womanhood.

"—!!"

This time, the math teacher silently threw a super-large protractor for blackboard use at the entrance of the faculty room. The door closed again, and the second teaching aid got stuck in it as well.

A quaking voice came in from the hallway. "I was just trying to explain why I came in before!!"

"It had better be worth making this situation so much worse. I demand a concise explanation of logical fact!!"

"Uh, the schools close down soon, so can we stop weeding now?"

"That was all?!"

Blood vessels appeared around Suama Oyafune's temples. She

grabbed a super-large compass for blackboard use from a desk, then burst out of the faculty room, ready to wallop the failure of a high schooler with it.

But Touma Kamijou wasn't there.

All she saw was a figure dashing around a corner and vanishing toward the stairs.

"What on earth is going on...?" muttered Suama, decidedly exhausted, but her voice went unheard.

7

"Crap...I really thought she was gonna kill me," muttered Kamijou to himself as he trudged home in the dying light.

With October starting, this time of day had been getting chillier, little by little. In response to the temperature change, there were somewhat fewer people around, too, compared to the summertime. The big screen on a blimp floating in the darkening sky featured a newscaster telling everyone to be careful with flames because the air was dry.

As Kamijou weaved around the cleaning robots ambling along the sidewalk, he wondered what he'd have for dinner, then decided to stop off at the department store by the station. He was a little worried about his refrigerator's contents. If he traveled a little farther away, there was a cheaper supermarket, but he'd be late getting home if he went there now. That would lead to Index, who was waiting in his dorm room, throwing a fit because she was hungry.

In any case, with the station close, he caught a glance of a brown-haired girl wearing a Tokiwadai uniform, facing away from him. It was Mikoto Misaka, he realized.

Moreover, she delivered a high kick to a juice vending machine, then started to wonder if *all* the machines in the area were malfunctioning...

When Kamijou saw that, he decided not to say anything and leave and promptly made a 180-degree turn. "...They say a wise man keeps away from danger. Also, to let sleeping dogs lie," he whispered to himself.

"Who says that?" came the answer from right behind him. He gave a jerk and went ramrod straight.

Cautiously, he made a second 180-degree turn to find Mikoto Misaka. Bewildered, he groaned in spite of himself. "Please spare me..."

"Again, from what?"

"Mr. Kamijou is extremely worn out from weeding after school and many other things! So please spare me any further trouble!!"

"What the heck are you even talking about?!"

As he tried to flee at Mach speed, Mikoto grabbed the back of his neck and snapped into his ear, "And would you stop trying to end all our conversations whenever you get the chance?! You never answered the text I sent you, and I want to see what happened to that, so let me see your cell phone!!"

"A text...? You sent one?"

"Yes!!"

Kamijou thought for a moment, then took out his cell phone, opened his mailbox in front of Mikoto, and looked at it askance. "...You did?"

"I just said yes!! Geh, your in-box is empty?! It's not treating my address as spam, is it?!"

Mikoto was astonished at this whole text thing, but then she arrived at another fact.

As Kamijou pressed the buttons, she clamped onto his hand to stop him, then peered at the names in his in-box folder.

"...Okay. Why, exactly, do you have my mom's number in here?"

"Huh?" *Come to think of it, I did run into drunk Misuzu Misaka in Academy City the other day...*

Mikoto, still frowning, used her thumb to control his cell phone, then called up the person in question.

"Wait, hey!"

It wasn't on speakerphone, but between the volume being turned up loud anyway and the short distance from him to her, he heard the call tone.

"Okay, *Mother*, I have something to ask you."

"*Huh?!*" came back Misuzu, sounding shocked. "*Is my display bugging out? My phone isn't showing your number, Mikoto.*"

Just from what Kamijou heard from their conversation, she seemed to ask how Misuzu ended up with his phone number.

"*Hmm...*" But Misuzu spoke slowly as she answered. "*I think I remember meeting that boy one night in Academy City, but...Mommy can't remember things from when she's drunk. Even Mommy doesn't know when any of this happened! Oh-ho-ho-ho.*"

"Mm-hmm, mm-hmm." Mikoto nodded before hanging up.

She smiled sweetly, closed the phone with both hands, and returned it.

"What...do...you...think you're doing, getting my mother drunk like that?!"

"What?! What kind of eccentric reasoning is that?! And I'm sure your mom remembers! That laugh at the end was too suspicious for her not to!!"

It only took a moment's thought to figure it out, but she seemed convinced that her little family was on the brink of destruction, since her face was bright red and she'd lost her cool.

Time for a change of subject!! thought Kamijou, deciding to take the plunge and steer the topic away through brute force. "C-come on. Mr. Kamijou has to go home and polish rice now...Wait, don't you have a curfew, too? The sun's already down!"

"What? Curfew? Easy to get past," she said flatly.

Kamijou was already feeling fed up with this conversation.

Mikoto, meanwhile, didn't seem to care about his mental health whatsoever, but the change in topic seemed to be successful. "The checks do feel like they've been getting stricter, though. Maybe because of all the stuff going on lately. Even people who never read the newspaper are all busy checking the news on their cell phone TVs and looking for info sites on the Internet."

"..."

"I guess everyone's worried, huh? ...*Especially after how it got like that before.*"

Mikoto was probably talking about September 30.

The incident that directly triggered the current "unseen war."

The incident where Academy City's gates were destroyed; residents all over the city, student and teacher alike, were systematically "attacked"; the peacekeeping groups Anti-Skill and Judgment were completely shut down; and a road demolished into a hundred-meter-long crater.

No one person was responsible for them all. Thanks to several organizations and opinions intersecting, not even Kamijou, who was directly involved, had a full view of it...Actually, he was starting to think *nobody* could understand the whole thing. And if a central figure felt that way, those who were only dragged into it would have pretty limited information.

Maybe the farther from the center one was, the more opportunity they had to observe from a safe location. And even Mikoto probably didn't take Academy City's announcement that "foreign religious groups were conducting scientific supernatural ability research in secret, and espers they'd developed were the attackers" at face value.

Mikoto looked away from Kamijou and stared off in the distance.

About five hundred meters from here was the street leveled by a certain great "angel's" appearance. Kamijou thought maybe she was thinking back to what happened on September 30, but she actually appeared to be gazing at the airship in the darkening skies. The giant screen attached to its side was running a news program right now.

"The large-scale Roman Orthodox demonstration and protest activity, which was limited to European nations until now, has begun in the United States."

The newscaster reading the script was calm.

"Today, protests have occurred in San Francisco and Los Angeles, shore cities on the West Coast, but they are predicted to spread throughout the entire country."

The image changed to what was probably Los Angeles. It would have been the middle of the night there, but the video took place during the day, so it must have been recorded.

Damn it. It made another big jump... Kamijou's face unconsciously twisted, like he was looking at terrible wounds.

As though a marathon had just started, an ocean of people was covering a big three-lane road. They were holding what appeared to be homemade Academy City banners, setting them on fire and holding them overhead or slashing through horizontal ones.

The idea was to tout how angry they were by marching down a mostly set route for hours. It wasn't like a riot, where everyone let their anger consume them and destroyed everything in sight.

But that didn't mean it was safe. The video showed a man bleeding from the head leaning against the side of an ambulance—there must have been a brawl. A sister, her face black-and-blue, was helping an exhausted priest to his feet, calling for help.

All of them were just normal people. None seemed related to anything like espers or sorcery.

Maybe, in a broad sense, the demonstrators were Roman Orthodox followers. Some would be wearing crosses around their necks, and others would be singing hymns from the Bible.

But unlike Vento of the Front, it was hard to imagine them being involved with the dark side of the religion. They went to their schools and jobs like normal people, and on days off, they would chill at home and have barbecues in their big backyards. That's all they were, really—wasn't it?

"...What is happening?" muttered Mikoto as she stared at the airship screen. "I don't know what happened on September 30, but we didn't want this, did we? They say that one incident triggered all this, but Academy City was minding its own business. Why are they fighting and hurting one another? The mastermind won't even show himself, either, so those people are the only ones suffering. Isn't that weird?"

"..."

Kamijou silently listened to her words.

A mastermind.

Mikoto had been using that term unconsciously. Part of that was probably hopeful: If someone was making everything worse, one just had to get rid of that someone and everything would go back to normal…Mikoto had raw power in the form of her Railgun, so maybe she found that easier to understand.

But there was no "mastermind" behind this.

Sure, certain people had been responsible for the incident on September 30 that started everything. Vento of the Front and Hyouka Kazakiri—plus whoever was behind them. Maybe if they could have stopped whoever that was on that day, they would have solved everything by "defeating the mastermind."

Still, in fire terms, it hadn't been kindling that started the damage. It was a giant wildfire, born as a result of something else. They were past the point where they could stop anything just by capturing the mastermind.

The demonstrators and protesters were completely normal people living over there. Nobody was ordering them, forcing them to do this. They'd seen the newspapers, seen news programs, and gotten angry, so they were participating in the protests—acting purely on individual beliefs.

To use the "defeat the mastermind" method to stop worldwide demonstrations, that meant beating up every single protester throughout the world.

They couldn't do that. Shouldn't.

But then how were they supposed to fix everything?

"…What's happening?" Mikoto repeated. Her words lodged in Kamijou's heart.

This wasn't something children would come up with an answer for.

INTERLUDE ONE

The Tower of Execution, also known as the Tower of London, was a tourist attraction in England.

Once it was said to be the end of the road for prisoners, a facility for blood and torture and beheading, one so harsh that people said that none who passed through its gates could return alive. Now, however, it was open to the public, and it was easy for anyone to take a field trip to it, costing a mere fourteen pounds—less money than going somewhere for afternoon tea. The exhibits showed both its history as a place of execution and many of the British royal family's jewels.

Meanwhile, however, an enormous blind spot lurked just out of sight, where its "facilities" were still operational.

It sat right next to the tourist attraction, but like a shadow cast by a bright light, one would never see nor enter this labyrinth from the outside. The dark group of facilities retained their past roles, which had given the building its "Tower of Execution" nickname—namely, capturing prisoners and, if necessary, torturing or even executing them without hesitation.

Enter from the front, and one would never see the shadows.

Enter from the back, and one would never escape them.

"…It's oppressive in here, as usual."

Stiyl Magnus muttered in spite of himself, as he breathed out a cloud of cigarette smoke. Unlike the touristy part, these more practical hallways were narrow and dark. Smoke from his lantern clung to the chaotically arranged stones in the walls, and with each flicker of the flame within, the human shadows it cast appeared to writhe. The floor was covered in a light layer of cold dew, as there were no systems to let moisture escape.

Then the girl walking beside him spoke. She was Sister Agnes Sanctis, a former Roman Orthodox nun.

"About this interrogation of Lidvia Lorenzetti and Biagio Busoni..."

"There are things I need to ask them about God's Right Seat," he replied. "If someone leading an entire force like you hasn't heard of them, asking a *VIP* would be faster."

"...Think they'll talk, those aristocrat priests?"

"Well, that's part of why I'm letting you see firsthand how we do things in England," he quipped. "It's too much effort to lecture every single person in your unit about it, though, so I'll leave that in your hands."

He stopped in front of one of the doors. It was thick and wooden, blackened, and weighed down by absorbed moisture. He opened it without knocking, then entered the quite cramped three-meter-square room beyond. This was still only an "interrogation" room, so the commonplace Inquisition torture devices were absent. The only things in the room were a table bolted to the floor and two chairs on either side of it, also secured in place.

The chairs on their right had minimal cushioning.

The chairs on the left, however, were exposed planks of coarse wood. Their armrests featured belts and metal fixtures, too—they were made for holding people's arms still.

And those two left-hand chairs did, in fact, have people bound to them.

Lidvia Lorenzetti.

Biagio Busoni.

Both were "high executives" in special positions in the Roman Orthodox Church.

Stiyl sat down in one of the chairs on the right and, sounding like this was a pain for him, said to them, "You know what I want to ask, yes?"

Agnes seemed to hesitate to sit down in the other chair; she remained standing next to him, looking uneasy with nothing to do.

Biagio, the middle-aged bishop anchored with belts and clasps to his chair, glared sharply at Stiyl. Agnes, formerly of the bishop's own cloth, winced even though the look wasn't directed at her, but Stiyl didn't seem to care.

Biagio's face was pallid; he had been sufficiently sleep-deprived to wear down his mind but not enough to damage his health. The shine in his hair and skin was gone as well. It was like he was steadily drying out.

"...What do you want to ask?" he said. "If you want a lecture on the Bible, leave it for Sunday."

"God's Right Seat. Tell me everything you know."

"Why don't you bring in those puritanical torture devices you're so proud of? Then I'll show you the depths of my faith, you inexperienced whelp."

Biagio maintained an insolent attitude. Lidvia, in the meantime, didn't seem interested in exchanging words at all. It wasn't that she was willing her emotions away; her expression was perfectly natural and unchanging. Biagio was letting his irritation show. Perhaps she was the one with more perseverance here.

Biagio's answer came as no surprise whatsoever. Agnes determined that this might take a while.

"Do not belittle Necessarius."

But Biagio wasn't the only arrogant one in the room.

Stiyl Magnus puffed out a thin cloud of smoke and smiled.

A chilling, brutal smile.

"I don't particularly care if you die during torture. Necessarius has ways of extracting information from the brains of corpses. Depending on protection and injuries, of course."

Those words were enough to shake even Agnes, standing nearby, to the core.

Biagio realized Stiyl wasn't bluffing and made a woefully bitter face. Lidvia seemed to finally take an interest as well—she glanced sharply over at Stiyl without moving her head.

The man didn't get particularly worked up over this; his voice was beleaguered, like he was staring down a pile of paperwork. "What I mean is, what you call 'torture' is a different beast than what we call 'torture.' None of this thinking it'll be easier if you died. I don't mind if you resist, but let me say that would be a waste of your lives."

Silence continued for a few seconds.

As Biagio kept his glare on Stiyl, Lidvia spoke readily. "*Such trivialities mean nothing to us,*" she said, looking straight at him. "That aside, there is one thing I'd like you to tell us, however. What is it like 'outside' right now?"

Stiyl frowned at that but remembered a moment later...*Come to think of it, I did get those reports, didn't I?*

From what he knew, Lidvia Lorenzetti was an eccentric even in the Church, one who only reached out to help people society couldn't accept. From her point of view, being locked in the Tower of London and not having the information she wanted from "outside" made her worry about those under her patronage. The fragments she'd caught about "worldwide chaos" served only to deepen her anxiety.

After thinking that far, Stiyl grinned.

Then he said, "*I'm sure you can guess.*"

Lidvia's expression twitched with a growl. It went without saying—the first victims of the revolts and disorder had been the weak ones.

"...Hmph."

On the other hand, Biagio Busoni had a strong sense of elitism, believing those in the priesthood were supreme. He seemed more interested in the fruits of the chaos than its harm.

Lidvia watched Stiyl. "In exchange for my cooperation, I request the release of my own who are currently being held in this tower. The release of people who can quell this chaos, even if only slightly, and build a roof over the heads of the weak."

However, it was Biagio who reacted to this, not Stiyl. He spat, not trying to hide his vexation.

Stiyl, meanwhile, was nothing if not relaxed. "You think I'll accept?"

"I will make you accept."

"And how?" he asked. The woman caught her breath.

As she sat there, both hands fixed to the armrests of her bolted-down chair, her lips began to move quickly.

"...*San Pietro elude le trappole dell'imperatore e del mago.*"

Stiyl frowned. They'd confiscated anything Lidvia could use as a Soul Arm or spell. No decent sorcery would activate just from a verbal incantation.

A light appeared anyway.

But not from Lidvia Lorenzetti.

It emanated from Agnes, as she stood next to Stiyl—more accurately, from the *cross hanging at her chest.*

"Damn!" Before Stiyl could react, a pillar of light flashed madly from the cross. It extended toward Lidvia in a straight line, destroying the belt and clasps holding her right arm down.

With that hand, she grabbed a sharp piece of broken metal from the ruins and thrust it at Stiyl's chest.

Slash!! Two hands intersected like bullets.

"..."

"..."

Stiyl and Lidvia remained silent.

Both had pressed something against the other's throat—Lidvia the metal fragment and Stiyl the corner of a rune card.

"—! Lidvia!!" Agnes recovered from her momentary shock and hurriedly grabbed the Lotus Wand from the wall she'd stood it against.

But Stiyl, still glaring at Lidvia, waved Agnes back with a hand.

The sorcerer was clearly having fun with this. As if to say *this* was what made it an interrogation.

"Did you think so little effort sufficient to take my life?"

"I have no other choice if you will not release those relevant," said Lidvia, her voice dispassionate. "Oriana Thomson. I request her release and that you let her lead away those overwhelmed by the revolts."

"Why don't you consider your position again?"

Stiyl's voice didn't shake, either. Oriana was the talented "smuggler" who had joined up with Lidvia.

"Your smuggler knows what's happening in the world right now, too. On top of that, she offered a deal—to have her mentor Lidvia Lorenzetti shelter the weak, and she's already agreed to temporarily cooperate with the Puritans. Tell me to release her all you want, but Oriana won't have any of it."

"…"

Lidvia and Oriana had both been thinking the same thing.

And Oriana had acted first.

Lidvia quieted, and Stiyl continued, "…Let's not let her resolve go to waste. If the Roman Orthodox Church—or rather, God's Right Seat—is creating this situation, there must be a clue as to how to overthrow them, correct?"

Lidvia didn't answer for a few moments. Biagio tsked and looked away, as if to say this was all a farce.

After a period of heavy, heavy silence, she slowly opened her eyes. "…What are you hoping to gain?"

"Necessarius's goal is explicit," he said wearily. "To save the lambs lost and engulfed by the overwhelming power of magic. That's what it was back then, and that's what it is now."

Lidvia stared sharply at him.

He didn't flinch.

Whatever she was searching for in Stiyl's expression, eventually she slowly exhaled and relaxed. "…I haven't met them directly," she said. "I *have* heard fragments of information by chance, however."

Lidvia Lorenzetti's words echoed through the dark interrogation chamber.

Next to Stiyl, Agnes finally took a seat and spread out a piece of parchment to record.

"According to that information, God's Right Seat is…"

CHAPTER 2

Deciding Trigger
Muzzle_of_a_Gun.

1

After Kamijou split up with Mikoto, he paid a visit to the department store near the station like he'd been meaning to. He peered into the fresh food section on the ground floor and saw that vegetables were cheap today, so he went in and bought about four days' worth of ingredients.

...Ready-made food seems really popular, but nobody's going for the ingredients like vegetables and meat and stuff. Maybe less people are cooking for themselves these days, he wondered as he left the store.

He looked up to see the airship still there, a news program on the screen on its side. Initially, he thought it would be more about the protests in the U.S.…but now it was on Russia. News about the demonstrations was the only thing going right now, so it was starting to get hard to tell what was new and what was old.

"…" Kamijou stopped and thought, grocery bags in both hands.

Something Mikoto Misaka said earlier was bothering him.

Demonstrations and protests happening throughout the world. These huge "incidents" weren't unmotivated—rather, there were so many motivations, they left no clues as to how to solve them.

The thing Mikoto was angriest about was having been used during the September 30 incident. The people of Academy City had done everything in their power, endeavoring to bring back the peace they used to have, but it had been used against them to help create new chaos.

Kamijou still wanted to do *something*.

Even Vento of the Front, who caused the upheaval, had her reasons. Even Hyouka Kazakiri, who stood at the crossroads of science and magic, didn't want this kind of discord. Outsiders, those whose names and faces they didn't even know, had butted in and made the world into this mess. That was wrong, no matter how one looked at it.

But…

What do I do…? Kamijou gritted his teeth as he stared at the airship floating in the sky. *I have to stop the problem. That's the biggest goal and easy to understand. But what am I actually supposed to do?*

Perhaps one way was to contact Tsuchimikado, who knew the inner workings of Academy City, or someone from the Puritan camp, like Kanzaki.

But now that the problems were so much bigger, Kamijou couldn't imagine any of them settling the situation at all. If pressed, he felt more like they were backstage specialists who took the initiative before the problems grew this large.

Anyway, standing around here isn't going to do me any good, he thought. *Still, I don't know how to contact the Puritan Church. I guess I'll go back to the dorm first and pay Tsuchimikado a visit, partly just to ask about that.*

And about how he skipped out on the weeding, too, he added inwardly. *Though maybe I've got it better than regular students just by having contact with an agent like him…?* He forced himself to think positively as he mused, walking down the dark streets again. Thinking in circles was making the grocery bags in his hands feel oddly heavy as he walked.

It was the homebound rush hour, so a lot of people were around.

Still, he felt like he was bumping into more people than usual. Going back to the dorm, getting dinner ready, and taking a bath was going to be a chore. *Wonder if there's any shortcut recipes that bypass the annoying parts, like using the microwave or rice cooker,* he thought with some seriousness. Normally, there was a chance Index surrendered to hunger and bit him if he took too long to make food.

As he wondered, he ran into another person walking. This time, it was an old woman about fifty or sixty years old.

"Whoops, sorry."

"No, don't be," said the old woman with an elegant smile, bowing her head to him instead.

She didn't walk hunched over, but even standing up straight she was two sizes smaller than Kamijou. A coat was folded over her bent arm. Plus, she wore a scarf around her neck, looking rather over-dressed for the beginning of October. *Maybe she's sensitive to the cold,* he thought idly.

The old woman brought her head back up and said in an unhurried tone, "I'm the one who should apologize."

"Oh, no, I'm the one who bumped into you."

"No, no, not about that." The old woman smiled.

Kamijou was about to frown before she spoke again.

"About the trouble I'm about to put you through."

He heard a soft metallic *click.* He looked toward the sound—near his stomach.

The old woman's arm was there. But with the folded coat hanging over it, everything from her elbow to the front of her wrist was covered with its thin fabric, completely out of sight.

All he understood was the feeling against his gut.

It felt like a hard, pointed stick. He cringed slightly.

"I really do apologize for this," said the old woman gently, bowing her head again.

2

Suddenly, Mikoto Misaka stopped.

Hmm...

She'd forgotten about it when she ran into that idiot, but now she remembered she had something to talk to him about.

...The Ichihanaran Festival.

Mikoto had a citywide cultural festival on her mind. This year's festival was still over a month away, but due to how terribly the Daihasei Festival, the aggregated athletic festival held in September, ended up (in reality, it was a succession of good, bad, and bittersweet, but she only felt it had been terrible), she'd been thinking about taking measures early for the Ichihanaran Festival.

Actually, half of that seven-day-long Daihasei Festival was one big string of problems related to that idiot. If I'd known it would end up like that, I would have taken the reins earlier...

When she said "taking measures," she meant, of course, securing from him a promise to go around the festival with her.

Why did it turn out like this? ...Well, I guess I can just call him, she thought noncommittally, taking out her cell phone.

She'd formed a pair contract with Kamijou on September 30, so his number was naturally registered in her phone. The whole setup was painful, but she had it, so she might as well use it. As she lined her cursor up on the number in her address book, her eyes went to the antenna symbol in the corner of her screen.

She was out of range.

"...!!"

She looked around, and though the road she was on wasn't small by any means, she ran all the way to a real main street, watching the antenna display at the edge of the screen. Then, after confirming she was having no reception issues, she brought the cursor to the entered number once again and pushed the Call button.

But all she got was an emotionless voice telling her the person she was trying to call was unreachable or his phone was off. This time, *he* was the one out of range.

"Urgh, this is hard to use…What's a cell phone good for if you can't talk to someone when you want to?!"

With anger on her face, she put her phone away, looked around, then ran off to search for him personally.

Not much time had passed since they'd parted.

The idiot was probably wandering around nearby anyway.

3

Kamijou and the elderly woman walked side by side down the street.

Many people were out and about, but nobody gave them a second thought. Anyone would see a high school student with grocery bags in his hands and an old woman with a coat draped over her arm and think they were completely harmless.

As Kamijou stared at her out of the corner of his eye, not bending his neck, she was the one to give a dry grin instead. "You don't need to be so nervous."

Having said that, though, she had already ordered him to turn his phone off and given him precise instructions on how quickly he should walk. Whatever was hidden under that coat, it was the real deal. He didn't know exactly what it was, but he clearly couldn't make a mistake here.

He considered waiting for a chance to jump at her and turn the situation around. *The problem is, I don't know what's really under there…If I do something careless and make things even worse, it wouldn't be funny.*

As Kamijou worried about this and that, the old woman quietly said, "Please act naturally. It isn't like I'm demanding you not move a finger."

"…Well, still…Why don't you bring out what's under your coat—?"

"*Ahchoo!*"

"Whoa!!"

The woman had suddenly sneezed, and Kamijou reflexively cried out. A group of students walking nearby glanced at them curiously, then continued on their way.

"I told you, it'll be all right. You've been so scared for a while. What is it?"

"Mainly the thing you're hiding in your coat!! What exactly are you sticking into me right now?!"

"Oh my. It's all right, everything's fine. It won't fire just because I sneezed."

"F-fire? It fires—you mean it really is one of those?!"

"It also makes a loud noise. Although I do have a little thing on it to make it quiet."

"That was a pretty huge hint!!" squealed Kamijou, trembling in fear. The older woman didn't worry about his shriek.

Escorted by her, they walked through a large shopping district and onto a side road. He realized they were heading for a part of town with a lot of student dormitories—though not the area his was in. Students made up 80 percent of Academy City, so admittedly "parts of town with a lot of student dormitories" were all over the place.

Where on earth are we going…?

If it had been a strange, abandoned factory or something, it would have maxed out his danger gauge. But that wasn't what it seemed like. Not with the scent of white stew for dinner coming from a nearby dorm and a group of elementary school girls secretly giving food to stray cats, as though making up for the fact that their dorm didn't allow pets.

As he was busy observing, the old woman stopped abruptly.

"Here it is. Right here."

"?" That wasn't enough for Kamijou to get it.

They'd come to a children's park.

It felt more like this place had been made because there was a little extra space left over from the buildings around it, not as an actual zoned park. It seemed somehow squeezed together, with the proper amount of playground equipment for a narrow area bundled into a set and shoved in.

But why, though??? Kamijou's mind reeled as he looked at the entrance to the empty space. It wasn't a special place. At least, not the kind where you'd hold an object against someone on the street and bring them there, prepared for them to see your face.

"I'm sorry. Please go in," said the old woman, ever so casually poking him with the thing in her coat.

He had no choice but to obey, but he still had no clue what all this was getting her.

At her instruction, they sat next to each other on a bench at the park's edge.

He initially suspected somebody else was waiting for them, or perhaps would be coming later, but that didn't seem to be the case.

Kamijou hunched over a bit and placed his two shopping bags on the ground. The woman didn't especially try to stop him. If he'd had a weapon in his shoe or something, maybe he'd be able to counterattack, but he wasn't armed to the teeth like some kind of ninja.

He also considered picking up a rock, but he had no clear opportunity to. If he messed up and made her more cautious, it would come to nothing anyway.

For now, he decided to give up and stand.

He asked the woman, "So what on earth are you trying to start here?"

"Oh, no. Nothing as important as you're thinking," she said with a sweet smile, poking him with the very much *important* object in her folded coat.

"Let's talk," she said.

"Talk?"

"Yes. About the chaos happening throughout the world right now."

4

She couldn't find that idiot anywhere.

"This is so strange…" Mikoto swerved onto a small road she'd already been down, looking to and fro, wondering where he was.

She didn't think it had been that long since they'd parted, but he wasn't at the place they'd last met. She'd searched several roads around that point, and still, he was nowhere to be found.

Maybe he'd gone into a store or something. Or maybe he'd gotten on public transit and gone somewhere?

...Where is that idiot's dormitory anyway? It's not like I'm a stalker. How am I supposed to know where to find him? They tended to run into each other without particularly wanting to, so he couldn't be very far away now. Thinking on it more, though, she had no idea where he even lived.

She folded her arms. *Well, the Ichihanaran Festival thing isn't urgent or anything, so I'll give up and go home for today.*

At least, she *tried* to brush off her irritation, but as soon as she spotted a side road out of the corner of her eye, she fidgeted.

...N-no, maybe one more road, she decided. Wondering if there were any roads around that she hadn't checked, she called up her GPS map on her cell phone—and just then, she spotted Kuroko Shirai among the crowds of homeward bound.

With a terrific *whoosh!!* she hid herself behind a building.

Wh-what? ...What am I hiding for?

It was a mystery even to Mikoto, but she vaguely felt like she couldn't let her twin-tailed underclassman find her just now. The other girl was a teleport esper, so if Mikoto was discovered, it would be really hard to shake her off on foot.

The Level Four Shirai was saying something to a girl next to her as they walked down the wide road. The girl had a voluminous crown of fake flowers on her head, so she was probably Kazari Uiharu from Judgment.

*...*Mikoto had the feeling that they were coming this way, so she entered the narrow road her hiding place had put her near. For now, she went farther and farther down.

And then she realized it:

Huh? ...Was this road always here???

She looked around closely again, realizing she didn't recognize the place. She'd thought she knew most of School District 7 by heart, but this was her first time coming here.

It was a typical Academy City residential area—not of apartment complexes and single-family houses, of course, but of crowded student dormitory blocks. It was filled with nothing but rectangular buildings five to ten stories tall, not big enough to be called high-rises. A garbage dumpster was set up directly under a wind turbine propeller. Maybe the propeller's movements were also used to keep pigeons and crows away.

All the meals at Tokiwadai Middle School were prepared by the school itself, so for Mikoto, the smells of dinner floating to her from nearby felt kind of fresh or something.

"…Well, this works. If I don't see him here, I'll call it quits for the day," she said vaguely, continuing her walk through the residential district.

5

Kamijou gazed at the old woman dubiously.

The chaos happening throughout the world…She could only have wanted to talk about one thing: the large-scale demonstrations and protests split between those on Academy City's side and those on the Vatican's.

However…

"…Talk about it?" he said. "There's nothing I can actually talk about to begin with."

"That isn't true. We need your opinion in order to solve this problem."

"My opinion? Not the opinion of some UN people or the president of another country?"

"Groups centered on the state have a tendency to be weak to religious and ideological strife," replied the woman easily and unexpectedly. "We commonly call these groups 'modern nations,' and it is quite rare that one solves problems like that. Many don't hesitate to *claim* they solved one, but most of the time, they are squashed with military force. Nations, in many cases, actually make the problems worse."

The old woman continued to speak, the park empty around them. Intellect came in many shapes and sizes, but hers was close to the teacherly kind.

"The chaos happening throughout the world right now is serious.

Nobody will be able to solve it easily, and it could also be the flame to spark a second conflict. If they fail to put the flame out correctly, they could cause internal strife severe enough to paralyze national functions. That's part of why no nation has carried out a military intervention against the demonstrations and protests. This is a difficult problem for them, and to be honest, nations would love to have a solution manual for it. Everybody is watching, waiting, until another country acts, so they can see what effects and results they achieve."

"...Who in the world *are* you?" asked Kamijou carefully.

The woman sitting beside him seemed a little different than other agents like Motoharu Tsuchimikado and Stiyl Magnus, who were armed for combat and assassination. And from her manner of talking, she almost sounded like an educator. But a mere teacher probably wouldn't make contact with him using a weapon hidden inside her coat.

...*She seems somehow different than the people I've met before,* he'd thought, so he'd cautiously put the question to her.

"Monaka Oyafune."

Her full name promptly came out.

"Maybe you'd understand if I said I was on the Academy City General Board."

It was one bombshell after another with this woman. "...What?" asked Kamijou in spite of himself.

The General Board was, so to speak, the highest agency in the sprawling Academy City—twelve people who focused on running the place. There was apparently someone even higher than them, a leader called the General Board chairperson, but nevertheless, the General Board's privileges were nothing to shake a stick at.

But at the same time...

...*Is she really one of those big shots?*

As one of only twelve members of Academy City's General Board, she could freely control Anti-Skill officers and private security police with a single command. It would be weird for her to come personally to talk to him, armed, and calling him to a tiny little children's park.

As Kamijou wondered in doubt, the woman who said her name was Monaka Oyafune smiled. "Is that not believable?"

"Yeah, um, it's just weird. Like that scarf around your neck, it's weird and shriveled—or, like, I get the sense that if you were on the General Board you could get a better one."

Kamijou was too confused to say anything sensible, but it startled Oyafune more than he expected. She suddenly brought a hand up to touch her scarf. "M-my daughter made this scarf for me. I will not let you insult it."

"O-oh," answered Kamijou with an awkward nod before thinking of another question. "Wait...I'm sure your daughter is a full-fledged adult at this point. But she doesn't seem very good at— Okay, I get it, I get it!! I won't mention it again!! I won't, so stop shaking whatever's inside your coat already!!"

Now he was being contained when he didn't need to be, so he decided to stop pointlessly exciting her.

Monaka Oyafune. The General Board...Those two pieces of information might not be correct, he concluded. *But maybe she's using a fake name so she can give me some kind of correct information. I don't like dancing in the palms of other people's hands, but I'll be the one to decide whether to dance and how.*

"...Anyway, you said you wanted to talk. About what?" he began.

Oyafune nodded, seeming happy. "A major problem is occurring throughout the world right now. A chain of disruptions with demonstrations and protests first and foremost."

"Well, I know that..."

"I want to ask you to solve it."

"How?" asked Kamijou, frowning at those sudden words. "If I could do it myself, I would. Wouldn't everyone in the world feel the same? But in reality, nothing's changed. Nothing is solved. Everyone knows we have to solve the problem, but nobody is trying. Do you know why?"

Kamijou continued, not waiting for an answer: "Because there's no simple reason or cause behind it. Nobody can solve a problem that doesn't have an answer. That's why nobody can do anything, even though the problem is being paraded right in front of them. It's just not solvable, is it? I hope you're not about to ask me to go around the world and talk down every single protester individually."

"What if," answered Monaka Oyafune, not backing down, as though she'd predicted that problem from the start, "there *was* a simple reason or cause? What would you do?"

"What?"

"This brings me to why I'm talking to you. I'm hoping for something that no United Nations or nation representative has—something that only you have."

"And what's that?"

"Your right hand."

"..."

Something only Touma Kamijou had. Without thinking, he glanced at it.

The Imagine Breaker.

It would be appropriate to consider for this. Whether sorcery or supernatural ability, the special power could erase anything related to any strange abilities. But for things that weren't, normal things like demonstrations or protests, it wouldn't have any effect. Which meant...

"Wait...*Is that how it is?*"

"It is."

"You're saying that a strange power is behind this chaos and that person is the cause of everything? And that if I destroy that one cause, everything will go back to normal? That if I act now, while it's still a continuing problem rather than a result of September 30, I can solve it?"

"*That's what I'm saying.*" Oyafune nodded simply. "By the way, Academy City isn't the one creating this discord. According to the chairperson, the Roman Orthodox Church, a religious organization, apparently possesses a scientific, supernatural Ability Development agency."

"...?" Kamijou almost frowned at that but then realized to the general public...or rather, by Academy City's announcements, sorcery didn't exist.

That was the story.

The idea of "sorcery" was what "scientific supernatural abilities" were called in ages past. It wouldn't do him any good to mention that here and now. If he interrupted without thinking, he'd just make the situation worse.

Oyafune, never letting go of her "scientific viewpoint," continued on. "Well—and this goes without saying—Academy City has no reason to sow discord. Naturally, if a problem has happened, it was the Roman Orthodox Church, not us."

"I see…" Kamijou almost agreed, but thinking calmly, something bothered him. "Wait, hold on. You're kidding, right? They don't gain anything from this, either. The demonstrations and protests are all happening in Roman Orthodox areas. The ones in the middle suffering because of it are people of that religion, aren't they? They can't benefit from making their own suffer."

"What if I said they *did* gain something?"

"…What?"

"It's simple," said Oyafune smoothly. "For example, official records state that there are over two billion Roman Orthodox followers. It's an incredible number, isn't it? Even all the children and elderly in Academy City combined only come to 2.3 million. If it came to a straight-up war, it would be a pure contest of numbers, and we would have no way to win. Even considering the geographical problems a war would pose for them, I'm pretty sure it won't make up for the numbers advantage."

"So what?" asked Kamijou.

"Oh, but don't you think that's strange?" she asked back. "The Vatican is currently making a serious effort to destroy Academy City. Why would they choose worldwide demonstrations and protests to do that? Why don't they take the simple approach and crush us with their numbers? Focusing everything on Academy City would be more effective than causing violence elsewhere in the world. Don't you think it's circuitous?"

"…You don't mean…"

"Yes." Oyafune smiled. "*The fact that they control two billion people is a lie.* If they could destroy this city, they would have done so long ago. Perhaps those people do wear Orthodox crosses, carry

Bibles, and go to church on Sundays. And maybe there really are two billion people like that in the world.

"However," she continued, "the issue is *whether they could commit murder in the name of Crossism*…and that makes things different. Though I'm sure there are people who would. Right now, the world is split in two: Academy City and a giant religious organization. But…what is the truth, really? Is there actually a clear-cut line in the sand?"

"…"

"Even people who go to worship on Sundays watch TV and use cell phones. Even athletes who train their body according to scientific sports medicine might pray to God during important games—that's what it's like outside Academy City in the so-called normal world. The lines are vague. People take the good parts from both sides, fortify it with their own beliefs, and then create their own worlds to live in."

"The science side and magic side…overlap…"

Oyafune knitted her brows and said, "Magic side…?" but still continued after a moment. "Yes. The world's great majority…the winners of its rule by majority—that's what it is. Everything is spread thin and wide. People will take out loans and plan their lives at banks managed by Academy City–related groups, then have their wedding ceremony in a Roman Orthodox Church…They're the ones populating the world: those who reap the benefits of both science and religion."

"Then…," said Kamijou. He felt the back of his throat starting to dry out, little by little. "The Roman Orthodox Church's goal…Wait, it's to get those people who reap the benefits of both science and religion to…?"

"Most likely. Having the best of both worlds concerns them. They want all two billion of those people secured. They want as many allies as they can get. So I believe they did *something*. And as a result, the cogs fell out of alignment and induced the demonstrations."

Something, she'd said. Was that the key to this incident?

"Inciting protests isn't what they're after. They want the boost from chaos to attack the foundation of the world Academy City's very existence has established."

Oyafune's words clearly came from someone on the science side. That bothered Kamijou a little, but there was no point arguing with her right now.

"Academy City is especially concerned by this part of what the Church is doing."

"Really…Because they're scared of all the people rallying to the Church because of the demonstrations?"

"That is one thing," admitted Oyafune, "but even if that didn't go their way, a different development is possible. We're currently in the middle of working out countermeasures to what we're calling *economic bombing.*"

"…Economic…bombing…?"

"The longer this chaos drags on, the worse the effect on our economy. It's dangerous, and it could trigger a worldwide scare. If that happens, then the Church wouldn't need to be big enough— Academy City could be torn apart."

Kamijou didn't quite get all this talk of economies and scares. He turned to the woman sitting next to him on the bench and said, "…These 'modern' nations you're talking about…Would they really fail that easily? They haven't been shaken at all yet, right? All this economics stuff—I don't know anything about money on the national level, but I can't see big armies getting ruined by business."

"If there is one representative or symbol of the scientific world outside of Academy City that's easy to understand…it would be so-called military powers. But even those nations have weaknesses to economic trends." She spoke slowly. "To maintain a military, you need tremendous capital. The worldwide chaos is limiting the sources of money they're using for that. In addition, no matter how small their income, the military always expends a certain amount of it. In other words, when an economic scare happens, military powers immediately take damage. The bigger the military, the more extreme their collapse is."

Is that real? thought Kamijou. A few countries like that came to mind, but they didn't seem like they would get jolted very easily.

"But those countries that have big militaries…Don't they have a ton of oil and lots of ammunition in store for times like these? Couldn't they go off that for a few years?"

"Ha-ha. Wars don't happen after reserves have actually depleted. Militaries wouldn't be able to fight at that point. If you can make them look at the current situation and think, *Eventually our reserves will run dry,* you can make them pull the trigger, and everything goes up in flames. And when a major power goes on a rampage—I think that's more than enough of a factor to tear apart the science world centered on Academy City."

Her strangely decisive tone struck Kamijou dumb. She probably had the numbers in her mind she needed to back that viewpoint up.

"I don't know if that process is related," said Oyafune, "but right now, Academy City is desperately trying to acquire war funds. Are they trying to make up for the numbers difference with cutting-edge equipment and unmanned weapons…or is there some other reason? We're holding weapons exhibitions, using the pretext of lowering our products' grade for the sake of mass production to manufacture 'mundane weapons' without actually using significant technology. Then we call them Academy City's newest weapons and sell them at high prices."

"…"

"Meanwhile, the Roman Orthodox Church is also amassing a war chest, in the form of contributions from the faithful. On the surface, they're peace funds to quell the chaos, and the people donating probably have no ulterior motives…but it's plain as day what the higher-ups mean when they say they'll use the money for peace."

The bigger the chaos got, the more funds they could raise.

The Roman Orthodox Church was enormous. With its two billion followers, even if everyone only donated one yen, they would have two billion yen. Of course, it wasn't compulsory, so plenty of people wouldn't donate, but wealthier strata apparently had a tradition of gaining status through how much money they donated. And going by what Oyafune said, they'd already gotten a lot more than two billion.

"Their system of indulgences is still around, though in a different form," said Oyafune.

Kamijou didn't really understand that. Was *indulgence* a historical term of some sort?

"You'd have to be quite the zealot to weigh science against religion and choose the latter. If someone told you heaven existed, you wouldn't decide dying was all right. Science is realistic, which means it's almost ridiculously easy to understand. People will flock to whatever's easy to understand. But there are people who still worry about it. And those are the people they did something to. Whatever it was, as I can see it, it affected the gears in their normally functioning minds and resulted in bringing about all this chaos."

"..."

Was this all true? For example, wasn't it possible Academy City caused this, not the Roman Orthodox Church? Academy City would have to fight the Church and its two billion followers with 2.3 million people. So they caused the chaos in the Church to whittle down the enemies' numbers a little. Wasn't that possible?

...This is hard.

The Roman Orthodox faithful were the ones central to the demonstrations and protests. But if they were spread thin like Monaka Oyafune claimed, they wouldn't be a direct combat force. And they wouldn't properly understand the sorcery aspect of the Church, either. It was hard to think about big shots like Agnes Sanctis or Biagio Busoni participating in the protests and rampaging around doing whatever they wanted.

If this was a plan of Academy City's, then it was hard to imagine it doing damage to their *actual* combat forces.

In fact, if the demonstrators were halfway between science and sorcery, then that would make them important people supporting capitalism. If they were too preoccupied with protests to do their actual jobs, that by itself would lead to economic damage. And if it was two billion people doing it, those losses would be no laughing matter. If they just wanted money for wartime, they wouldn't purposely constrict their own sources of funds.

If there was some kind of conspiracy going on behind the scenes,

Kamijou decided that it would be appropriate to think the Church had caused this chaos—to win over the people on the fence.

And when things came to the dark side of the Church, Imagine Breaker likewise became more valuable.

"But still," he began after thinking it through, "let's say the Roman Orthodox Church was doing something, and they were related to some kind of trick or whatever. What on earth would the trick be? My power doesn't amount to much. I don't know where they are or what they're using. It's not a convenient tool I can use to meddle in things like this. If I'm going to cause trouble, I'd at least want someone to take me to the stage."

"Yes. About that—" began Monaka Oyafune before stopping.

A new figure had appeared in the small children's park.

"Tsuchimikado?" muttered Kamijou, seeing his sunglasses-covered face.

It was Motoharu Tsuchimikado, his classmate. He should have been at school after it ended, but he'd vanished when it came time to do the weeding. Kamijou considered griping about that, but this was clearly neither the time nor the place. He couldn't—not with the way he seemed.

The air about Tsuchimikado was completely different from how it usually was.

"...Finished talking?"

He didn't speak to Kamijou. His eyes, behind his blue-lensed sunglasses, were only looking at Monaka Oyafune.

Oyafune, for her part, wasn't surprised. Maybe she was acquainted with the agent known as Motoharu Tsuchimikado. "We are not, but this is fine," she said. "If you're to be the one, I can accept that."

"I see," said Tsuchimikado shortly before exhaling quietly as if he was bored with an annoying job. "You've taken care of business?"

"I did yesterday."

"Then I'll start, if you don't mind."

"There is nothing you need to hesitate about," answered Oyafune with a smile.

Tsuchimikado looked slightly away from her. He reached behind him and took out something from the belt of his pants.

"Tsu...chimikado?"

There, as they left the confused Kamijou out of the conversation, he saw something unbelievable. A black, shining metal item in Tsuchimikado's right hand. An object just fifteen centimeters long. It was...

...*a pistol?*

Though his mind caught up, Kamijou couldn't stop him.

Not because he couldn't predict what was going to happen.

But because even if he had predicted it, he didn't believe his classmate could follow through with such a heinous thing.

Bang!! The dry gunshot echoed through the tiny park.

Monaka Oyafune, nevertheless, was smiling.

Her body wavered, then fell off the bench and onto the dirt.

6

Mikoto startled at the loud noise.

It sounded like the crack of gunfire.

The shrill noise drilled into her ears, then echoed into the air.

Wha...? What was that???

Fireworks? But October wasn't the season for them. In terms of other possibilities, maybe a fire-creating esper had done something...?

She heard several windows opening in the student dorms nearby. With such a loud sound, they must have been worried. None of the students went so far as to leave the building, though; it seemed spectating didn't hold enough interest if it meant interrupting dinner.

Guess an esper's going crazy. Well, this just turned into a chore, she thought, heading in that direction.

She was a Level Five electromaster, the Railgun. She could handle most espers on her own, one way or another, and was confident that if dragged into an incident, she could turn the tables. Even if someone threw her into the middle of a fight between a berserk esper and Anti-Skill, she'd probably return unharmed.

Still, even she had once faced *a problem she couldn't do anything about alone*, but...

...!! *Th-that's only because the two key people were way too irregular! And that doesn't have anything to do with this! A-anyway, I'll go see what I can find over there. Um, which way was it again?*

Mikoto shook her head, focused, and started walking toward the noise.

All she could see in this seemingly normal neighborhood was student housing to every side.

7

Monaka Oyafune had been shot in the gut.

It took several seconds for Kamijou to realize that fact.

Motoharu Tsuchimikado had shot her.

It took another few seconds for him to process that.

Oyafune hadn't resisted. She'd been poking Kamijou with something in her coat before, but he never saw her point it at Tsuchimikado. She knew exactly what was coming and took the bullet anyway. Such was the scene before him.

Tsu...chi...mika...do?

Kamijou's gaze slowly moved away from the fallen Oyafune.

Tsuchimikado's expression remained the same.

White smoke still billowed from the pistol in his right hand. He brought it behind him, then hid it between his shirt hem and his pants belt, picked up the empty shell casing from the ground, and put it into his pocket.

All of those were completely calm, simple actions to him.

That made Kamijou explode.

"Tsuchimikadoooooooooooooooooooooooooooooooo!!"

He shot off the bench and grabbed his classmate's shirt. When he saw that the eyes behind the sunglasses still didn't change in the slightest, Kamijou clenched his fist and threw a punch. He felt the

uniquely dull sensation in his fingers and wrist joints as he connected. Hit in the face, Tsuchimikado reeled back, and he fell to the ground. But even after falling over, his expression remained the same. He clearly didn't feel any of the damage whatsoever.

This bastard!! Kamijou clenched his teeth and took another step forward.

But then he received interference—

A small hand weakly grabbing his ankle.

It was Monaka Oyafune's, even though she'd just been shot.

"...Don't...," she said, lips touching the dirt as they moved. "Please...don't blame him..."

Those words were enough to throw Kamijou into confusion.

Monaka Oyafune continued.

Smiling.

As though thankful Kamijou had stood up for her.

"My actions...don't match...the ideas...of the rest of the General Board...representing Academy City..."

"What?"

"They want the war to get worse...They want to destroy...*the other science side called religion*...represented by the Vatican...They want to take advantage...of this chaos. They don't...want this to be... resolved so easily..."

Kamijou looked at Tsuchimikado again. As always, his face was still, like he'd known everything since the beginning.

"Making the war worse...It's absurd...You must stop it," she said slowly, her voice tinged with pain. "But a board member...can only...use so much authority. I can't...do it. Someone who went against the head's will...and lost her power because of it...can't do very much. So I...had to contact someone. Someone...who could actually...fix the situation..."

She was looking at Kamijou. Gazing into his eyes as she spoke.

"...One day...this contact will be revealed. The plan was...that I would be punished...for my rebellion. Alone...I could have avoided this...but then others would be punished."

Others, thought Kamijou, a chill running up his spine. "If you ran, they would go after your family...?"

"..."

Oyafune didn't answer. Her silence stated that she didn't want anyone to worry about her.

"...I'm the one...who asked him," she said instead. "Just to clarify... he said no. So please, don't...blame him...I'm the one who...made the difficult request...that he enact my 'punishment'...but miss my vitals..."

"Don't talk," interrupted Motoharu Tsuchimikado finally.

He slowly got off the ground and peered into the old woman's face.

Kamijou couldn't see his expression from here. Tsuchimikado probably didn't want to show it, either.

"We'll do the rest. You've done your duty well. I know you have a lot more to say, but I only have one answer for you. Don't worry. That's all you need to remember."

After Tsuchimikado spoke, Oyafune's smile slowly deepened. Around her neck was a homemade scarf, not very well-made. That was her reason to fight.

Stopping the conflict between Academy City and the Roman Orthodox Church, making sure not to have anyone else perform her "punishment"—it all came down to that. Tsuchimikado crouched and searched through her belongings, then took out a cell phone and called an ambulance. After wiping off the fingerprints, he put it on the ground.

Then Tsuchimikado took something out of Monaka Oyafune's coat.

It looked like a small pistol for self-protection. He stuck it behind his belt and then looked at Kamijou. "Can you move right now, Kammy?"

"Yeah, I get it," he said through clenched teeth, staring at the fool of a woman lying on the ground. "...She set up all this, this outrageous nonsense, so I would do something. Just so I would do something. You have to be kidding. How indirect can you possibly be?"

Touma Kamijou wasn't a person of any particular renown.

If she'd wanted him to do something, all she had to do was talk down to him and not let him answer.

The thought made him grip his right hand.

"I'll explain later. We don't have time," said Tsuchimikado. "We're going to District 23. There's a plane ready. Monaka Oyafune prepared it with her power just for this. I'm not about to let that go to waste."

"This…is bullshit…," muttered Kamijou as he followed Tsuchimikado out of the children's park.

The only thing they left behind in the park was a blood-covered Monaka Oyafune.

As he listened to the ambulance sirens in the distance, his jaw was tight.

8

What Mikoto Misaka found was a small children's park.

The place looked like they'd been building the dormitories nearby, but they had space left over, so they'd made it into a park…rather than having planned it out beforehand.

Several vehicles were parked outside the entrance.

They were Anti-Skill's.

Mikoto was about to get a closer look when a man dressed in black blocked her way like a wall. Several layers of yellow tape blocked off the entrance as well, cordoning off the space.

She glimpsed inside the park.

There were several Anti-Skill men, like the one blocking her now, huddled together, but no other "normal person" was present. They were clustered near a bench at the park's edge and seemed to be investigating something.

She didn't know what had happened.

She didn't know what had happened, but it looked like it was already over.

INTERLUDE TWO

"...God's Right Seat apparently exists to overcome original sin."

Lidvia Lorenzetti's voice echoed through the interrogation room in the Tower of London.

Stiyl and Agnes, listening carefully, both raised an eyebrow. Nothing was more familiar to a Crossist disciple than original sin.

"The sin Adam and Eve received when they ate the fruit of knowledge...and the sin all of humanity bears as their children."

"That is the Old Testament's say on the matter," Lidvia noted. "In the New Testament, the Son of God takes on the role of erasing sin. When he was crucified on the cross, he single-handedly took all humanity's sin upon himself to erase it all. Because of this, all who pray to the cross, eat the body and drink the blood of Christ at Mass, and continue to be faithful until their very last moments...Their sin will be washed away at the hour of judgment and they will be led to heaven. That's the idea anyway.

"...However," she said with a pause, "there are exceptions to this."

"Exceptions?" repeated Agnes as she compiled a record on a piece of parchment. Stiyl glared at her, but the conversation proceeded.

"Yes, an exception to the sin given to all of humanity..."

"The Virgin Mary," finished Stiyl, finding the answer already.

Biagio, fastened to the chair next to Lidvia's, tsked quietly.

Regardless, Stiyl continued, "As the vessel who gave birth to the

Son of God, she was in deep contact with the Holy Spirit, and her sin disappeared. The Immaculate Conception, as it's called. In other words, original sin didn't exist for Mary. Even though all of humanity are Adam and Eve's children and shoulder their original sin, and that property should have been passed on to the child as well."

"Which means there are exceptions," agreed Lidvia. "To begin with, in the New Testament, the Son of God walked the path to his execution precisely because there was no other way to cleanse original sin than for him to shoulder it. If one considers that, along with the fact that the sin vanished from the Virgin Mary, I believe the answer follows naturally."

"...That there's some other way to erase original sin rather than staying faithful to the Son of God?"

"A spell to trick it, as it were. I've heard God's Right Seat has succeeded in weakening their sin as much as possible, but they haven't yet been able to erase it completely."

Though bound to her chair, she spoke so calmly that it was questionable if she even felt the restraints.

"However, though their erasure of their sin is imperfect, they have apparently gained magical knowledge surpassing normal humans. As it goes, they can even cast spells that utilize angels and kings, ones said to be impossible for 'humans' normally."

"...Well, man's end goal is to erase original sin, after all. If that were possible, the very qualities that make us human would shift and become something closer to an angel. But..."

"Yes. Original sin is synonymous with the fruit of knowledge, and losing it means normal sorcerers would lose the ability to use normal magic...A special property, if you will."

"Hmm." Stiyl exhaled slightly.

Erasing original sin.

An idea kept in the deepest annals of Crossism's largest denomination, Roman Orthodoxy; it seemed incredibly appropriate to call it a bomb.

In Crossism, it was believed that true happiness was achieved through the expunging of original sin by constant devotion, then being guided to God's new holy land after the Last Judgment. Dedicating their days to researching esoteric methods to get rid of original sin was very Roman Orthodox of them.

After summing his thoughts up, he pressed on with Lidvia: "Which means God's Right Seat's endgame is to completely erase what little original sin still remains in their bodies...Is that so?"

If they succeeded, God's Right Seat would truly be able to freely use angelic spells. If that happened, even saints wouldn't be able to stop them.

"Heh-heh." Lidvia chuckled.

"Am I wrong?"

"You are. For God's Right Seat, erasing original sin is nothing but a means to an end. Their final goal is something else."

"...Fully removing original sin is just insane. And now you're telling me that's only a *means*?"

Then what the devil is their real goal?

Lidvia smiled quietly. "They've flaunted their goal from the very beginning."

"What?"

"...God's Right Seat. That is their destination."

CHAPTER 3

Far from a Sorcerer

Power_Instigation.

1

Academy City School District 23.

Specializing solely in the aviation and space industries, all the important airports in the city converged there.

This district lacked the crowded high-rise landscapes of the others, featuring only rows upon rows of runways and rocket launch sites. Flat asphalt went on as far as the eye could see, with control towers and experimental stations sparsely dotting the ground.

Kamijou stepped off the train and onto the platform, staring out at the scenery. "It's like a ranch made of stone and iron..."

They'd fought Oriana Thomson here during the Daihasei Festival as well, but he was getting the impression that security today was even tighter than it had been then.

He went over to the station's coin lockers to stow the grocery bags in his hands. All the lockers in the city were airtight, and they even had refrigeration and freezing options. Probably thanks to all the scientists here.

Still...

"...Man, that's expensive. How is this a normal price for one hour?!"

"Meowsa. Seems more economical to just get rid of your groceries now, then visit a cheap supermarket tomorrow and buy more."

Tsuchimikado had a point, but Kamijou didn't feel like letting food go to waste. After putting everything in a locker and giving his fingerprint to lock it, he decided to turn on the refrigeration function and left.

As he walked through the station toward the exit, he asked his classmate, "If we're in District 23, does that mean we're going on an airplane?"

"Well, yeah. We're going to another country, after all."

"Seriously?! …Wait, do we have passports?"

"Nope," came the immediate, curt reply.

Kamijou grew quiet.

Tsuchimikado droned on, "It's not like we're going overseas for a vacation, boyo. This'll all be off the books. If they find us out, we're in for some international criticism. We're nyaat gonna get anywhere if we whine about getting a couple of emigration stamps."

"O-oh."

There was a lot Kamijou wanted to ask, but Tsuchimikado had been so up front with him that he had to wonder if his way wasn't actually better.

Outside the station, there was a large-scale bus terminal. In general, one didn't walk around District 23; they used regulated buses. Tsuchimikado picked out a bus headed for an international airport and climbed aboard. Kamijou followed suit.

The roads in District 23 were mostly straight, it being no buildings and all runways. The speed limit was pretty lax here, too—they passed a road sign saying any speed up to one hundred kilometers per hour was okay.

Out his window were plains made of asphalt, and even the horizon was constructed and gray. From beyond the horizon, he could see white steam spouting up and forming cumulonimbus clouds.

A low rumbling noise turned into a quake, quickly making the windows rattle.

Tsuchimikado stared in that direction, muttering, "A rocket, huh? Looks like it launched safely, nyo?"

Kamijou took out his phone and turned on the TV app. The news was showing a rocket launch from various angles. "They're saying it's the fourth satellite Academy City has made," he murmured. "Wonder what the truth is."

"One thing they're after by launching a rocket now is making everyone else start to ask questions. They'll guess anything—from the city launching military satellites to testing ICBMs...The more possibilities are out there, the better we can probably hold everyone else in check, nya~."

So this is what an information war is like..., thought Kamijou, only to have a realization strike him. "...Huh. Now that I think about her, what about Index?" He was opposed to taking her into danger, but nonetheless, he worried about leaving her alone in a room without any food.

"That's all right, Kammy—Maika's gonna be going to your room. Her usual gluttonous face is probably glowing thirty percent brighter right about meow~."

On one hand, that was a relief. On the other, he was taken aback; had the meaning of his existence been reduced to "guy who made food for Index"?

In the meantime, the bus pulled up in front of the international airport. As Kamijou got off onto the asphalt, he checked the time on his cell phone. "Hey, Tsuchimikado. By the way, where are we going?"

"France," answered Tsuchimikado offhandedly.

"*Ugeh?!* Europe? Another long trip...Wait, how many nights are we staying there? And we'll be on the plane for a pretty long time... About ten hours?"

"Nah, we'll get there in a little over one, nya know~?"

"Huh?" blurted out Kamijou. It was a mysterious declaration.

Tsuchimikado seemed to think explaining would be a hassle, so he pointed toward a runway somewhat farther away from the airport terminal. Several large passenger planes, each dozens of meters in length, sat parked in a row. "Look, we're getting on one of them~."

"...You're kidding me," said Kamijou, nearly speechless, asking his friend for confirmation. He'd been on one of those planes once before. "Um, *that* kind of plane? If I recall correctly, the kind we used to get back to Japan from Venice…"

"Yep, seems like it, nya. I didn't have much to do with the *Queen of the Adriatic* incident, so I don't know the details."

"…*the kind that can go seven thousand kilometers per hour?*"

"Ha-ha-ha," laughed Tsuchimikado. "Everything's better faster, right?"

"This is way too fast!! Don't you get it? When you're in one of them, it feels like a thick iron plate is slowly crushing your body! Index was finally starting to open her heart to science a little bit, but after riding in one of those, she locked up her shutters tight!!"

He had another anecdote: Despite the situation, she'd unreasonably ordered an in-flight meal, which proceeded to end up all over the wall behind them in a magnificent scattershot.

"Please. Kammy, this is unofficial foreign work. You didn't think we'd be taking our time getting to France, eating some in-flight meals and watching movies, did you?"

"W-well, I guess that wouldn't feel very urgent…Wait, we're seriously getting on one of them? M-Mr. Kamijou doesn't really think he can recommend that!!"

"It'll be fine. Once we get past Mach 3, your amateur's senses won't know the difference, nya~."

"What the heck part of that is supposed to be fine?!"

Despite his weary complaints, Tsuchimikado didn't pay attention; he just said, "We'll talk on the plane."

The young man couldn't do anything if these were the only planes available to them. After he led Kamijou past business-use doors and roads instead of using any typical gates, they headed for the supersonic passenger jets.

2

"A Soul Arm called the document—that's the key this time, nya."

Tsuchimikado's words echoed through the spacious interior.

The supersonic passenger plane was a size bigger than normal jumbo jets. Aside from the crew, they were the only two using it right now, and that made it feel big enough to inspire loneliness.

Since they were the only ones aboard anyway, Kamijou and Tsuchimikado sat right in the middle of first class. Unlike the packed-in economy class seats, these had enough space to stretch one's legs and then some.

In that plane, Tsuchimikado looked at Kamijou from the next seat over. "Its full name is the Document of Constantine," he said. "Back when Crossism had just started, they faced persecution by the Roman Empire. The first emperor of Rome to officially acknowledge the religion was Emperor Constantine. The document is something he wrote for the Roman Orthodox Church's benefit."

The conversation wasn't the kind friendly classmates had with one another. Motoharu Tsuchimikado had already become a sorcerer.

"They wrote in the document that the Roman pope was the highest authority of Crossism and that Constantine would give the right to all of the land he governed in Europe to the Roman pope. Basically, most of Europe belonged to Emperor Constantine, and he handed over possession of it to the Roman pope and told everyone who lived there to follow Roman Orthodoxy...A certificate suspiciously good for the Roman Orthodox Church."

As Tsuchimikado spoke, he fiddled with the touch screen LCD next to his seat.

"As for its power as a Soul Arm...Yeah, it's said to be like a compass. If you use the document anywhere inside the lands Emperor Constantine governed 1,700 years ago, it still displays a seal that says this land is a legacy of said emperor to this day. Since it treats his legacy as belonging to the Church, it follows that the Church retains sole authority regarding the development and usage of any land or item its seal reacts to, nya."

He peered at Kamijou's face from the next seat over. "Kammy, are you listening to me like you're supposed to, nya?"

"*Oghghghghghghhhhhghghghoghghoghghohhbhbffght!!*"

Kamijou couldn't answer the question.

Seven thousand kilometers per hour.

The massive g-force that speed created was crushing Touma Kamijou's internal organs. He wasn't exactly in a condition to talk. An analogy might be someone pushing a basketball into one's gut, then also stomping on it from above as hard as they could.

Tsuchimikado, nonchalant about the whole situation, was the abnormal one here. "Okay, fine. I'll just keep talking."

"Ugehgh!!"

As Tsuchimikado listened to Kamijou's garbled grunts, indistinguishable between answers and groans, he calmly continued, "Like I said before, it's *really* fishy if the document was even authentic. Actually, scholars in the fifteenth century declared it was a fake. Even practically speaking, it was a lie. The document's true power—its power as a Soul Arm—*wasn't nearly that weak.*"

"Gigigighhhhghuughh!!"

"Its real powers are way more wide reaching. It actually has the power to make anything the Roman pope says into 'correct information,'" he said with whispered smoothness. "For example, if the pope declared that such and such a religion was disturbing the peace and was the enemy of mankind, it would become absolutely correct that very instant. If he announced that if you prayed to God and put your hands on a burning metal plate, you wouldn't get burned, then they'd actually believe that, even without any justification."

"Ooohhhhhhheehhheeee!!"

"Hey, Kammy, could you look at me when I'm talking to you, nya?"

Kamijou's upper body jerked and twitched. Still, somehow he managed to croak out a few words. "Document…usage…an'thng pope sez…all…b'comz correct…yah?"

He seemed to have kept up with the conversation, so he must have been listening, even in the current situation. This was Kamijou's last resort—figuring it would be easier on him to talk than to stay quiet.

"So then…izzit like…alch'mist's…Ars Magna…grant any…wish… *ohwhh!!*"

"No, it's not like that, nyo~," said Tsuchimikado in a cheerful voice, like he might start humming a tune. "Its only effect is that it makes people *believe* something is correct. It just makes them think the pope can't possibly say anything wrong, no matter how ridiculous it is, you knyow? It won't actually change the laws of nature or anything."

He fiddled with the small monitor attached to his seat's armrest.

"Plus, the Soul Arm only makes those of the Church believe something is 'correct.' It can't control anyone who couldn't care less about what the Church thinks is right or who didn't mind being wrong in the first place. For better or worse, it's a Soul Arm that exists for the Church, nya."

"A-a-a Soul Arm...makes th'ngz...he says...correct...? B-but that...*urbh!*"

"Ha-ha. Maybe it sounds cowardly, nya. But back in the days, where what important people said was absolute law, they had plenty of *little tricks to maintain their dignity.* After all, people would only trust what an important person said as absolute law if they had dignity, nya. If that trust was shaken, the entire country would be in a dangerous situation...Remember how in Japan, during the Edo period, we had a system where samurai were allowed to kill people in the streets if they thought they were being insulted? If a commoner said one bad thing about a samurai, they ended up in two pieces. If that's not the simplest example of restricting freedom of speech, I don't know what is, nya."

"Then...th-the-the-the-then...they made...the doc'ment b'cause..."

"Because they were scared, probably. Of the world they'd built shaking and swaying...And the Church did face its share of crises. In Crossism, God is absolute, and God was supposed to save people from all of that. But in reality, the bubonic plague wiped out half of Europe and the Crusades were a complete failure, and at the time, they never knew when the Ottoman Empire's main forces would press into Europe."

Tsuchimikado's voice was entirely impassive. But his face was showing a little something like sympathy.

"...The idea that God is absolute was shaken many times over.

But the Roman Orthodox Church had to persist in the belief. That's why they needed the document. Faced with such a grave threat, they wanted to keep the people's hearts close. That's what the document was for."

It was, so to speak, a Soul Arm to bridge the gap between ideals and reality.

By forcing people to believe, it protected their hopes.

It seemed incredibly ugly and, at the same time, done out of good intentions.

S-s-so the Roman Orthodox Church is using the document now to..., thought Kamijou, taking deep breaths, *...to make people believe the statement that Academy City is bad is "correct"...And that's why these twisted "demonstrations" are happening—because they forced the idea into their brains.*

Kamijou moved his lips, blue from the g-force, and asked a question. "B-b-b-b-b-but if they...had that crrr'zy Soul Arm...why d'dn't...use it...till now...?"

"Because its powers are immense. Once it defines something as 'correct,' it's hard to take it back, even by using the Soul Arm again. They can't just go around defining anything they want as 'correct' without forethought."

Tsuchimikado's answer was swift.

"And it's not easy to use. Remember how I said it makes people think what the pope says is 'correct,' nya? Not everyone can use it, and you have to be in the right place. Originally you couldn't use it unless it was set in the heart of the Vatican. From there, the order goes along ley lines and out to the whole world."

"H-huh? B-but...we're going...get in the way...'f it...right now...?"

"Yep."

"Wh-why...France? You just said...can't use...unless...Vatican..."

"Huh? Oh, right. About that..."

"A-also...if you use...doc'ment...can't cancel...right? Can we... stop that...errselves?"

"Well, you see, nya...I'll need to explain that, but where should I start...?"

As Tsuchimikado was about to continue, a soft electronic beep came over the plane's speakers. After that, a computerized female voice made an announcement. It was in a foreign language, but it didn't seem like simple English. Tsuchimikado listened, then made a face.

"...Oops, looks like we're out of time. Kammy, are you sure you're okay? If it hurts, try taking deep breaths. Breathe in..."

"Shh..."

"...and out."

"...haa."

"And in again..."

"Shh..."

"...and out again."

"...haa."

While they did that, Kamijou somehow was feeling better...or at least, he thought he was. But as Tsuchimikado peered at his face, his friend's expression was still clouding over.

"Gah, this is gonna be a pain, nya. Wasn't breathing out supposed to make it easier? Come on, Kammy, I'll guide you, so come over here. Push the button on your seat belt to undo it. There's no flight attendants here, so no need to worry, nya."

Tsuchimikado casually rose from his seat, and Kamijou wobbled up after him. He wasn't really going under his own volition so much as he felt like his mostly hazed-over mind was piloting his body of its own accord.

Kamijou's guide walked down the passage and opened a door, then walked down another smaller passage and slipped through a hatch short enough to accidentally bump his head, until he finally reached a place with exposed metal that was...roaring, for some reason.

Wait, where were they?

As Kamijou stood there dazed, Tsuchimikado pushed some kind of backpack at him.

"Here, put this on."

"??? Tsuchimikado? Um, what did you mean by exhaling making it easier?"

"It'll be fine, all right? It'll open soon. Quick, put it on."

Tsuchimikado was already putting his backpack's straps around him. The thing was indiscriminate, with straps not only on either shoulder but also around his stomach and chest.

Kamijou didn't really understand but watched him do it, then closed up his own straps.

"Great. Kammy, you look good, too, nya." Tsuchimikado slapped a big button the size of a can lid on the wall. "Make sure you breathe out all the way before we go!!"

Kamijou heard a strange booming noise.

A moment after he realized it was some sort of thick pump going…

Ga-clat!

Suddenly, the airplane's wall opened wide, and he saw the blue skies beyond.

"I…uh?" His pupils turned into little dots.

And then a wind so fierce whipped into the airplane, telling him this wasn't the time for making cartoonish faces. Almost immediately, everything seemed to be on the verge of being expelled from the plane.

"Tsu-Tsu-Tsu-Tsu-Tsu-Tsu-Tsuchimikadooooo?!"

Kamijou quickly grabbed the parts of the wall that jutted out with both hands. But he didn't know how long he'd last.

As the wind roared around them, the other youth smirked. "It's time, Kammy. If you're ready, let yourself loose and breathe out, nya!"

"Don't '*breathe out, nya*' me!! The hell?! D-did…did you just fling open the rear cargo haaaatch?"

"Well, we can't just land in a French airport like idiots. Those Roman Orthodox assholes would find out, you knyow? This plane is headed for London. We're getting off partway through the trip."

"Are you a moron?! Think about how fast this plane is going! If you opened a hatch going over seven thousand kilometers per hour, it would wreck the inside of the plane!!"

"Sorry. It's already open."

"I'm dead!!"

"Don't be silly, Kammy. If I really did that, I wouldn't be this relaxed."

...Could this plane have actually slowed down for this emergency drop-off...? he wondered. It would make sense since he hadn't been feeling sick from the effects of the g-force...

"Y-you...Then why did you tell me to take deep breaths?! That didn't mean anything, did it?!"

"Come on now, Kammy. You can't struggle forever. Let go of the wall already."

"I was thankful. I really was! Thankful to you, Tsuchimikado, for being so considerate to me!! I can't believe you did this!!"

"Shut up. We're going."

Tsuchimikado kicked his hands off the dents in the wall—and the spiky-haired boy lost all his support.

The fierce winds blowing through the plane immediately picked up Touma Kamijou's body, and he passed through the cargo-loading hatch on the fly and tumbled out into the skies.

It was afternoon, local time.

The sky was pure and blue and punctuated by a high school boy's shriek.

"Ugyaaaaaaaaaaaaaaaaaahhhhhhhhhhhhhhhhhhhhhhhhhhhh!!"

A 360-degree view of blue sky unfolded before him.

Wh-what's happening? Just a few hours ago I was having a forkball contest with Fukiyose. Why the hell did I just get dropped out of a plane above France?!

As he spun so fast he couldn't tell up from down, he saw Tsuchimikado smile like he was truly enjoying this sky sport and jump right out of the plane.

I'll kill you...You piece of shit, when we land, I'm going to beat you into a bloody pulp!!

Then he paled. *...Wait, are we even gonna land somewhere safe?* he thought, and a moment later, there was an explosion as his backpack burst apart.

The giant parachute inside expanded. It must have been made to deploy automatically when it reached a certain speed.

Unfortunately for Kamijou, it had come as a complete surprise.

"Gehhh?! M-my neck...can't bre—"

He didn't have a chance to finish his complaint.

*Plop...*His arms and legs dangled limply, and in an extremely unnatural position, the boy continued his descent.

Incidentally, the wind blew his parachute far from his intended landing position, eventually grounding him right in the middle of the Rhone's one-hundred-meter span. But he didn't know that yet.

3

Kamijou heard a watery squelch.

When he realized it had come out of his own mouth, it alarmed him.

His parachute had drifted along with the wind, dropping him in the middle of a river. It didn't feel like his legs were touching the bottom. He wasn't particularly good at swimming, but he was no slouch, either. Still, underwater with his clothes on and with the big fabric sheets of the parachute tangled around him, his body was sinking so fast it was almost funny.

He didn't see any signs of Tsuchimikado landing nearby. They might have gotten separated. Kamijou didn't have time to bother with that, though, since he was underwater.

He couldn't tell how deep the river actually went. It was possible it was surprisingly shallow, but with his current distress, it was more than enough to drown him. All the water gave him right now was fear.

He used his hands to try and paddle; they moved a few times slower than he thought. And his arms were trembling. Muscle fatigue, shaking from temperature loss due to the cold water, fear that he'd never go above surface again...

All those things muddled together, making him feel like something invisible was squeezing him more and more.

Crap, he thought.

The air stored in his mouth sputtered out like someone had wrenched it open from inside.

He looked overhead and saw the sunlight glittering on the water's surface. A mad dance of light, dulling his sense of distance.

Oh yeah, I got flung into the water from the ice ship in Chioggia, Italy, too, he thought, feeling a strange sense of déjà vu as he stared at the surface.

…Then all of a sudden, something broke it with a huge splash of bubbles.

…*!!*

Before Kamijou had the time to be surprised, a slender arm reached out of the curtain of white air for him.

By the time he realized someone had jumped in, the pale hand had grabbed his arm.

Yoink.

It began to haul him upward. His body, in its state of odd relaxation, approached the surface, reeled in as if by a rope. It took less than ten seconds for his face to break out of the water and touch air.

He heard the water splash loudly.

He'd yearned for this oxygen so much, and yet now he couldn't breathe much in. Something was wrong with the muscles that moved his throat or lungs.

"Are…are you all right?!" came a girl's voice from immediately next to him.

The parachute was like a weight, still dragging him down, down into the depths. Having to support the weight of two people, the girl's voice raised even higher.

"We're going to…bank. Please stay relaxed!!"

The riverbank…It was more like a shallow, dry section of riverbed. When they got there, Kamijou fell onto his rear end. Not only were his clothes wet but the parachute fabric had also absorbed water, making his body feel incredibly heavy. Plus, while he'd been struggling underwater, the chute's strings had gotten wrapped around him, and now they were nothing but shackles.

"Is…Do you do it like this.．.?"

The girl reached to him from the side.

With a loud *ka-click*, he was finally released from his bindings.

Having escaped the entwining parachute, Kamijou slowly gained his feet on the river sand, which was underneath water about as deep as a puddle.

He looked overhead and saw that the sun was high in the sky, which probably meant it was after noon. There was nobody else around but the two of them, though. Maybe they were all afraid of protests and riots and weren't leaving their houses today.

He took a look around. Right nearby, there was an arched stone bridge. However, it was half-destroyed, crumbling and cut off mid-river. Maybe the girl had jumped into the river from there.

Right, the girl. He looked at his savior.

He was supposedly in France right now, but she was a Japanese girl. She was probably about his age. Black, shoulder-length hair, distinctive double-edged eyelids, a pink tank top, white shorts ending above her knees. All in all, she cut a slender figure.

"Did you inhale any water…?" she said, peering into his face with a look of consideration. Then he recalled who she was.

*If I remember right…*He coughed. "You're from Amakusa… Itsuwa, was it?"

"Um, yes. It's been a long time," she said, cutely bowing her head.

But she, along with the rest of the Amakusa members, was supposed to be living in London right now. They wouldn't be in France for no particular reason.

Why is Itsuwa here? He wondered for a moment. *Wait, in this case, I guess there's only one reason…*

"Hey, Itsuwa. Did Tsuchimikado call you out here?"

"I…um. Mr. Tsuchimikado?"

Contrary to his expectations, Itsuwa gave him a blank look and crooked her head to the side.

He coughed again. *Wait, was I wrong?* he thought, blinking in surprise. "Well, I mean. All that stuff about the worldwide demonstrations and protests, and the Roman Orthodox Church's Document of Constantine having something to do with it…"

"H-how do you know that?" cried Itsuwa, putting a hand to her mouth. "Y-yes, we're currently investigating the document. But Amakusa spent so much time looking for that clue. How do you know so easily?! I should have expected no less from the one who punched our former priestess to the ground with one fist!!"

Itsuwa's eyes started glittering for some reason, but the amnesiac Kamijou didn't have those memories. He only wondered with a little fright, *Seriously, what the heck did I do to Kanzaki?*

Meanwhile, Itsuwa presented him with another commonsense question. "Um, well, that is…Wait, why did you suddenly fall here with a parachute in the first place? Shouldn't you be at school in Japan?"

Kamijou scratched his head, wet with slightly muddy water. "Well, I came here with Tsuchimikado to stop the document…Did he not instruct the Puritans to tell you what he was doing?"

"The English Puritan Church is the one who made this request of us—to look into the magical value of the ley lines and geography of France."

"Huh," he muttered, then blinked. *"Us?"*

"Yes," said Itsuwa with a small nod. "All fifty-two of the Amakusa-Style Crossist Church's combat personnel are mobilized, investigating France's main cities. I was assigned here to Avignon, but…Then you fell from the sky, and I didn't really know what was going on…"

"…I see. This city is named Avignon?" he repeated dumbly.

Kamijou had been dragged and dropped from the airplane by Tsuchimikado, and so he hadn't known where he was currently. When he thought about it, maybe he should consider himself lucky for running into a familiar Japanese face here.

Whatever the case, if Tsuchimikado planned on coming to Avignon the whole time, it was highly probable the Roman Orthodox Church was using the document right here.

Which made this enemy territory.

And Kamijou had fallen right into the middle of it.

"Hey, by the way, Itsuwa. I think Tsuchimikado was saying they had to be in the Vatican to use the document, right?"

"Y-yes."

"Then why are we investigating France and not Italy? I asked him, too, but he knocked me out of the airplane before answering."

Itsuwa must have thought the last part was a strange joke. She made a quite oddly pained grin.

Then she gave a start, remembering something. "Oh, um, could I go grab my things before we talk about that?"

"What things?"

"I left them on the bridge. I-I'm a little worried about someone stealing them."

The bridge must have been the one right nearby—arched and made of half-destroyed stone.

Itsuwa must have really jumped into the river from there.

"Oh. It's a little late, but thanks. If you hadn't saved me, I would have been in serious trouble."

"N-no, not at all! I didn't do much!!" Itsuwa's head whipped from side to side as she waved a hand in front of her face. Flecks of water flew from her hands.

After seeing that, Kamijou asked another question. "Oh, right, Itsuwa, do you have a change of clothes in your bag?"

"Huh? W-well, Amakusa is a religion specializing in covert activities, after all..." Itsuwa was surprised at the sudden question, but her expression as she explained herself seemed somehow prideful. "I left most of my things for this stay in the hotel, but I have a complete set of clothes for tailing or fleeing in there. I didn't have a chance to use it until now, though."

"I see. That's good."

"?" Itsuwa looked at him blankly, evidently not realizing what Kamijou was actually talking about.

But he couldn't just say it to her directly.

Instead, he looked away and into the sky, using his index finger to point.

"..."

Itsuwa saw where he was indicating, and glanced in that direction...

...to her chest.

And to her pink tank top, which water had soaked into, causing its colors to bleed and the fabric to stick to her skin, showing the entirety of her silhouette.

4

Incidentally, this Itsuwa girl seemed to have a very peaceful, conscientious personality.

Even when Kamijou bluntly pointed out the situation, she didn't karate chop him, bite him in the head, or try to burn him to a crisp with a one-billion-volt current, or anything eccentric like that. Her face had reddened as she gave a painful grin, saying something like, "Ah-ah-ha-ha. Well now, this is rather embarrassing. Ah-ha-ha-ha-ha-ha," crossing her hands over her chest, and trotting away to the bridge with her bag on it and her change of clothes.

Her face was smiling, but her eyes seemed strangely tearful. She seemed like an adult, one with very good sense.

"Hmm…" For some reason, Kamijou was the one feeling super awkward. *She could have at least yelled "kyaa" or something,* he thought, gazing into the distance.

After about ten minutes, Itsuwa returned wearing completely different clothes. Where on earth had she changed? She was perfectly dry now, but he sniffed faint perfume on her—maybe she was worried about the smell of river water.

"I-I'm sorry I made you wait," she said. She had a big bag over her shoulder.

Her clothing consisted of a blouse that was light green like ice cream and dark brown pants that went down to her calves. Her blouse looked thin enough to be see-through if one held it up to the sun. Itsuwa didn't have the buttons done up; instead it was tied in a knot near her navel to hold it closed.

Directly over her naked upper body.

She wasn't wearing anything underneath, which seemed, strangely enough, to emphasize her cleavage.

Kamijou gave her a blank look. "…Itsuwa?"

"I—I can't help it! This was supposed to be worn over my tank top to change the impression my clothes gave! Please don't say anything, please!!"

She was right; it must have been for slipping on, because upon closer inspection, the blouse had no buttons. There was no way to close it except for tying it in the front.

She seemed well aware there was only so far she could go with what she had on hand. She withered under Kamijou's indefinable gaze.

But originally, Itsuwa had jumped into the river to rescue him. He would just have to back her up for now.

Kamijou set his lacking brain into full motion. "But Kanzaki wears something like that, so isn't it okay?"

"The priestess does *not* dress this slovenly!!" Her complete denial was also a reaffirmation that her own clothes were so, and her entire face went red.

Still, if she was brazen about it like Kanzaki, she could probably pass as a "girl who probably was out dancing all night long." But she was being coy about it, huddling up and fidgeting, which made her stand out as unusual.

"Well, I don't know about Mr. Tsuchimikado, but if you're here to get the document, too, shall we meet up with him and act in concert?" She must have wanted to get the idea of her wardrobe off the table quickly, because the topic shift had come with some force.

Kamijou, for his part, knew absolutely nothing about French. He had no passport, either, so he had no way of getting back to Japan if he ended up by himself. Itsuwa's proposition worked all of that out.

"W-well, I'd appreciate it."

"Then let's go somewhere we can sit down first," she suggested. "There's a lot we have to talk about."

Kamijou looked down at his own clothes. "I'm soaking wet," he muttered. "It'd be nice to at least wipe off the mud."

Itsuwa's spine straightened. She began to fish through her bag, flustered. "I-if you need it, I—I have a hand towel right here."

Before she finished talking, a towel slapped over his face.

Kamijou turned back, surprised, to see an older Caucasian man walking a big dog along the dry riverbed as he waved his hand behind him without looking, as if bothered and saying, "I don't need it back."

Kamijou took the towel off his head. "...Right. Guess there are nice people out there. Why do French people look so cool when they do simple stuff like that? Huh? Itsuwa, why are you all frozen up?"

"N-nothing, it's nothing...," she replied, shoulders drooping.

He tilted his head in confusion as he continued wiping up the dirt on his face and clothes with the towel. "Which reminds me. There's demonstrations and riots happening here, too, aren't there? Do people get inspected? I don't have a passport or anything."

"There have been several inspections but only of possessions. I don't think they were serious enough to ask people to show passports. And I can trick the searches by using sorcery," she added, then muttered quietly, "A bigger towel. That was a good idea. B-but no, hand towels are good, too...," as she readjusted her bag's shoulder strap.

Avignon.

A city in the south of France. The original, ancient town, four miles across, sat at the heart of the modern city, surrounded by ramparts. Many a building was crammed into the limited space there. During its golden age, it must have had a big effect on European culture as a whole. Perhaps that was why it was France's number one tourist location to this day.

"...Hmm. Anyway, you said you were investigating the Document of Constantine in Avignon. I get that, Itsuwa, but..."

After receiving that explanation, Kamijou and Itsuwa passed through an arched castle gate installed in a giant stone wall, then entered the ancient boundaries of Avignon.

When they came out into what looked like a public plaza, they saw something like an open café. Its signboard sat beside the road, with French words (or what Kamijou had to assume were French words) next to the English on it. It didn't feel as much meant for tourists as just made in consideration of people there for the first time.

Itsuwa led Kamijou out of the public square and onto a smaller road. *Maybe she's got a hole-in-the-wall place*, he thought. "I thought we were going somewhere to sit down for now."

"Y-yes."

"So why are we going to a Melty Coffee? I mean, it's a foreign business to begin with, so it's not weird it's in France, but I thought it was entirely a Japanese chain. Isn't there, like…you know, a famous hidden place some old couple started up as a hobby or something?"

"W-well, there are some places like that, I suppose…," said Itsuwa apologetically. "Um, those places mostly have only locals going there…If Japanese people from abroad like us went in, we'd really stand out. I figured, well, a chain restaurant like this where lots of Japanese tourists visited would be better…"

"Mm," grunted Kamijou. He was about to yield to her opinion but suddenly thought of something. "…Wait, Itsuwa. If we're worried about appearances, I'm pretty dirty right now."

Kamijou had gotten a towel at the dry riverbed earlier, but that alone couldn't get all the dirt off. His clothes were a lot drier, but he couldn't do anything about the mud stains.

"If I go in like this, we might not just stand out; they might chase us away, right…?"

"No, that's all right," replied Itsuwa in a natural tone. "*Right now, that's all right.*"

He understood what she meant as soon as they entered the store.

Its interior furnishings were exactly the same as the ones in Japan. The entire wall facing the road was a glass pane, with seats for one and longer tables lined up in rows. In the middle of the room there were four-person booths, with the ordering counter in the back. Kamijou couldn't read French, but given the omnipresent placards with no-smoking symbols on them, these were the no-smoking seats. But if there was one difference, it would be the patrons. Since this was France, of course, he didn't see any Japanese people.

Nobody had been around where he'd landed in his parachute, but the café was fairly crowded. Perhaps it was simply that while people were afraid of the protests and riots, they couldn't stay cooped up at home and still live their lives. The point was that the flow of people was extremely focused, since they were only going to places they absolutely had to.

And there was one other thing.

Most of the guests had mussed hair and dirty clothes, mud on them, and arms and legs wrapped in bandages. Everyone from the burly adults to the small children had at least a bruise on their face, with uninjured people being more unusual.

"Protests and riots, huh...?" muttered Kamijou to himself.

For the time being, though Academy City and the Roman Orthodox Church were displaying completely antagonistic viewpoints, it hadn't escalated into full-blown military action. Still, these changes were steadily starting to eat away at the world.

Unpleasant changes—changes nobody wanted.

"We have to do something soon," said Itsuwa softly.

"...Yeah. Hence the strategy meeting." Kamijou kept his answer short as well.

This wasn't the time to be relaxing and eating, but Itsuwa pointed out that if they sat around without ordering anything, they'd stand out. Well, Kamijou found it uncomfortable indeed to make small talk under the glare of the employees, so they went up to the counter for now.

The lady behind the register was, of course, French.

Okay, thought Kamijou. "I-Itsuwa, since we're in France, do I have to speak French?"

"What?"

"Like, should I be expecting some plot twist where even though she's French, she can speak English?"

"Um, I think English should work in most places in the EU. Japan is surrounded by water, but here their sense of national borders is weak. See, look—that man over there is German, and the one across from him looks Italian. The chain restaurant service business needs employees to talk to a lot of different people, so I don't think French is the only thing that will work here."

"O-oh!!" said Kamijou, getting energetic all at once.

The time had come to show them the fruits of using his "Easy English Training" cell phone learning application. In truth, he was stuck on practice level four in the app, but no point worrying about that. He marched right up to the counter, and before the cashier could ask what he would like, he said, "*Coffee and sandwich please!!*" in English.

His English was mostly just him pronouncing the words with Japanese sounds, but the lady nodded in understanding.

Sh-she understood!!

…Being overjoyed at this made him feel like his practical English level didn't amount to very much. Then the lady said something in a foreign language that meant something like, "That will be seven euros."

Kamijou lost his calm.

He couldn't pay in yen.

"What…what now…?!"

As Kamijou's face darkened like lightning had struck it, Itsuwa held out a few paper euro notes from next to him. He told her he'd pay her back later, then started wondering how many yen were in one euro.

Itsuwa, in Japanese, said to the cashier, "U-um, I'll have an espresso and a Berkshire pork sandwich and also a bag of Healthy Vegetable Sticks, please."

The French cashier nodded again.

Kamijou couldn't help but shout, "What? Japanese?! I could have spoken Japanese?!"

When he looked at the cashier more closely, he saw many small badges in the shapes of national flags attached to her uniform, near her shoulder. They were probably signs that a customer could use any of those countries' languages.

When it came to that, Kamijou's English ability only became even more dubious. The cashier could have just understood the Japanese-pronounced words and put in the order from that.

Now quite disheartened, he took the tray with his order on it and went to get a table. Itsuwa came a few moments later. She first placed her own tray on the table, then took her bag off her shoulder and put it at her feet.

When she did, he heard a heavy metallic *clang* from the bag.

"…?" Vaguely interested, he looked that way.

When he did, Itsuwa blushed for some reason and waved her hands in front of her. "P-please don't worry about it!"

"But, well…"

Before Kamijou could continue, Itsuwa said without moving her lips almost at all, "(…It's a weapon.)"

"Huh?"

"(…The handle is split in five pieces. To use it, I connect them all to make a spear. I know using 'joints' makes it less durable, but I can't carry it around unless I do…)"

Now that she mentioned it, he thought he remembered Itsuwa using a huge spear in Chioggia, too.

"Anyway, um, did you get in touch with Tsuchimikado?"

"No." Kamijou took his phone out of his pocket. "…Haven't heard from him since we got separated while falling. I just can't get through. My phone's working, so he probably either has his phone off or isn't near any ground antennae…Anyway, I think he'll be fine no matter what happens."

He tested it once more, but it didn't even seem to call, probably because one of them was out of range. *I'm surprised it survived falling in the river. This thing is tough*, he thought, returning it to his pocket.

For now, he figured he'd eat his sandwich and have this strategy meeting. But then, he realized there were no napkins on his tray. "Eek, now what? I wanted to wipe my hands off before eating."

For some reason, Itsuwa's eyes sparkled at his complaint. "I-i-i-if you need one, I have a..." She blushed and started fishing through the bag at her feet, but a French waitress suddenly passed by them, curtly said "sorry" in what must have been French, and very rudely slammed a few napkins down on the table.

In front of Kamijou, Itsuwa—who was in the process of taking out a hand towel—stopped moving in pure disappointment.

As Kamijou wiped off his hands with the napkins that finally got there, he broached the main topic. "By the way, about before, you said you were investigating Avignon...Wait, what's wrong, Itsuwa?"

"N-no...nothing...," she said, wilting like a leafy plant left unattended on a summer windowsill.

He pulled himself together and tried again: "You've been investigating stuff about Avignon, right? Why France and not the Vatican? Did you find something suspicious?"

"Y-yes," said Itsuwa with a nod. "I was actually going to contact the others from Amakusa in France after getting a little more information."

"Which means we were spot on," suggested Kamijou.

Itsuwa didn't deny it. "Do you know of a building called the Papal Palace?"

"?"

"It's the largest Roman Orthodox building here in Avignon. Actually, it's more correct to say the city of Avignon expanded out from that building."

"Papal Palace, huh...?" he muttered. Papal—did that mean the pope? "Hm? But wouldn't a palace for the pope be in the Vatican? It sounds like the most hoity-toity name they could think of."

"Well, you see," Itsuwa began, seeming a little troubled for words. "The city of Avignon has a somewhat complex past."

"What kind of past?"

"At the end of the twelfth century, the Roman Orthodox pope and the king of France had a dispute. France won the dispute in the end. The king of France apparently won the right to make several demands of the pope at the time...One of them was for him to leave his headquarters and come to France.

"It was called the Avignon papacy," she added. "And also the Babylonian Captivity."

"The headquarters—you mean the Vatican?"

"N-no. I think it was called the Papal States at the time."

Anyway, she went on to say that France wanted the Roman papacy under their control to use the Roman Orthodox Church's various privileges and favor.

"And they chose Avignon here as their place of confinement. So the palace they locked them up in was given the name the Papal Palace, or the *Palais des Papes* in French."

"Locked up, huh?"

"Several Roman popes were held by the Babylonian Captivity for sixty-eight years. Of course, they still had to do their job as pope in the meantime." Itsuwa munched on a vegetable stick. "But as the pope, there were things they couldn't do outside of their headquarters, the Roman Papal States. I suppose appointing new cardinals and ecumenical councils were the big ones. The Papal States' location, the buildings there, and all the Soul Arms within…They couldn't re-create all the same conditions in Avignon.

"That would be the same as making an entirely new version of the Papal States," she said. "So, the Church needed a trick."

"A trick?"

"They couldn't create the same facilities in Avignon as back home. Instead, they built magical pipelines between there and Avignon, allowing them to remotely control the facilities in the States."

"…Like connecting an access computer to a big server."

"When the captivity ended and the pope returned to the base in France, they supposedly severed the pipelines several times…But considering the local ground current patterns, that seems like the only building in Avignon they could use the document from. Maybe the current Church reconnected the pipelines at some point."

"Hmm…" Kamijou nodded. After thinking about everything for a few moments, he said, "Did you investigate inside the Papal Palace?"

"N-no," said Itsuwa, wincing and shaking her head. "I'm just snooping around, that's all…Originally, the plan was to get enough information first and contact the vicar pope, then get a big force here and go in together."

Apparently, the vicar pope, Saiji Tatemiya, had received a "special Soul Arm" handed down through Amakusa. Still, now that the document was involving the entire world, Itsuwa decided that acting alone was a bad plan.

"If Tsuchimikado is trying to get here, too, you'll have another person saying Avignon is suspicious, a different information source. That means, like you suspected, it's very possible the Roman Orthodox guys are using the document in the Papal Palace.

"But...," he added, "it originally belonged to the Church, right?"

"Y-yes."

"Then why not the Papal States...er, the Vatican, I should say...? Why don't they just use it there? I don't see any special reason to take it out of their base. Avignon is just for remote controlling Vatican facilities, not for sorcery they can only do in Avignon."

"I have a few theories about that, but..." Itsuwa thought for a moment, then slowly continued. "I wonder if it takes a huge amount of time to get permission to use it. The one hundred and forty-one cardinals at the top of the Church have to all agree on it. The pope has great authority in the Vatican, but I still don't think he could use it arbitrarily. I think that's also why they couldn't be reckless with it before."

Itsuwa explained that even the upper echelon of the Roman Orthodox Church had its turf wars, so the arrangement was probably to avoid using the document for those purposes.

"However, we have information saying control through Avignon is irregular and doesn't need the agreement of all the cardinals. But in exchange for activating it outside the Vatican, they can't do it instantly—they seem to need preparations in Avignon. To be blunt, if we act now, we might still be able to stop them from using it and calm the chaos throughout the world."

"But either way, we can't do anything without investigating the Papal Palace..."

"I—I almost have enough information for Amakusa to act. I think we should begin our charge on the Papal Palace in a few days."

In a "war" that was a confrontation of science and sorcery…it seemed Itsuwa and the others would fight to stop the Roman Orthodox Church.

The English church probably didn't appreciate the Roman church at the helm for the sorcery side. Still, they didn't want to make trouble by openly opposing them. She used the word *Amakusa*, but never the *English Puritan Church*. Which meant that they were using Amakusa, under their umbrella, to obstruct the document. And if Amakusa failed, they could claim that a smaller faction of theirs were acting on their own accord, with no connection to the Puritans' intentions as a whole.

"…"

Kamijou had already been separated from Tsuchimikado. Instead of going by himself to the recognizably suspicious Papal Palace and upsetting the situation, he felt like acting in tandem with Itsuwa and helping Amakusa with their plans was more reliable.

For Kamijou, it was simply more efficient to help Itsuwa gather information so Amakusa could break into the place. "Itsuwa, is there anything I could help with?"

"Huh?"

"You said you'd rush the palace in a few days, but the sooner the better, right?"

"Y-yes," she said, trying to answer despite her confusion. "If you want—"

But he didn't get to hear the whole thing.

Because, with a dull roar…

…the window facing the road suddenly shattered all at once.

It hadn't been a thrown rock. And not a bat or metal pipe, either. It was hands.

Dozens, hundreds of human hands had pressed against the glass, and their pressure had caused it to shatter inwards. He heard several shrieks in the store, but even that was drowned out by a vortex of people flooding inside. It was like a horror scene in a zombie movie.

It was clearly abnormal, but Kamijou knew the cause immediately.

"A riot?!"

"Th-this way!!"

Itsuwa grabbed her things at her feet with one hand, Kamijou's arm with the other, and immediately ran. They went toward the emergency exit rather than the front entrance. Meanwhile, a throng in the hundreds entered the shop, very quickly transforming it into a jam-packed space like a full train car.

<"Japanese people!">

<"From Academy City?!">

<"Kill them. Don't hesitate. They're the enemy!!">

Kamijou didn't know a lick of French, but the emotion in their voices rang strangely clear in his ears.

He turned around behind him. Several screams overlapped. There were women and children inside, too. But before he could go back for them, Itsuwa had kicked the emergency door closed.

"Itsuwa!!"

"The way they're moving, nobody will die. There are too many of them. The rioters are restricting their own movement. As long as they don't start falling over like dominoes, nobody will be seriously hurt."

"That's not the problem!! At least the children—"

"Is that all?!" Itsuwa shouted, interrupting him. "...If that's all, then that's happening all over the world. And what do you think we could do if we went back into that human wave? We came this far so we could pull this disaster out by the roots as soon as possible, right...?"

"...Damn it."

"If we can just do something about the document the Church is using, this will quiet down. If we get caught in the riots, we won't be able to move. And then there won't be anyone to quiet them down."

"...Goddamn it!!" he spat, grinding his teeth. *The Roman Orthodox Church is making all the riots they want, and Academy City won't do anything about it so they can use it to their advantage,* he thought. *And the only ones suffering in the end are the ones caught*

in the middle! How am I supposed to ignore this? I'll stop it right now.
I'll stop this stupid nonsense as soon as I can, I swear!!

Kamijou and Itsuwa ran down a back road, towered over by buildings on either side. Somewhere behind them, a large man shouted. The sound of glass breaking found its way to their ears. And whose shrill crying was that? Even an explosion shook the air; someone must have lit some gasoline.

He couldn't figure out the goal of this.

Were they after a Japanese business chain in Avignon? Did they want to attack a hotel with a lot of Japanese tourists inside? Whatever the case was, they'd already forgotten their original purpose, and now the streets were flooded by people who just wanted to go on a rampage.

"Itsuwa, how far are we running?"

"For now, we just have to get somewhere we won't be caught by the—"

Her words suddenly cut off.

She'd just seen a new crowd on the other side of this narrow street.

...Such perfect timing..., thought Kamijou, his shoulders giving a jerk. "Hey, Itsuwa, you've been looking around here a while, right? Ever been caught in a riot like this before?"

"Huh? N-no. Amakusa specializes in blending in with their environment. Normally, we see beforehand when a riot is going to happen and then leave the area before that..."

"...Thought so." That informed Kamijou of an unpleasant fact. "Their timing is too good."

"What do you...?"

"If we assume the enemy using the document is hiding in Avignon like us, they might have seen me falling with my parachute. Even if they didn't get a clear look, they should have been able to detect a supersonic passenger plane made in Academy City slowing down and air-dropping something. If they're on the lookout for me, this kind of reaction makes sense."

"Wait, so..."

"These riots…They're intercepting us!!" cried Kamijou, just as the crowd blocking the road started moving toward them.

The old city of Avignon, where the Papal Palace was, was small, closed in by these old ramparts. They'd kept on putting buildings in this already limited space, and the paths were so small even bicycles had trouble getting through. Add to that the ten-plus-meter-tall buildings towering over them, and all this city gave him was a bizarre sense of oppression.

Their narrow road was blocked in several places by the human hordes.

Those participating in the riot actually looked like they were hurting themselves physically.

Kamijou thought for a moment, then made up his mind. If they didn't go against the flow of the crowds in front of them and break through, they'd never reach the Papal Palace. And at any rate, if they didn't go there, the problem would remain unsolved. The longer time dragged on, the more everyone got hurt.

"Let's go, Itsuwa."

"Huh…?"

"Doesn't look like we have time to wait for Tsuchimikado to call. Amakusa won't be here right away, either, right? We should squeeze by them and go for the palace. Now that the enemy knows about us, even they might not be around for long."

And…

"In the worst case, they might still be able to use the document if they go back to the Vatican. Even an amateur like me knows this'll get worse if they take it back to their base. We need to wreck that thing here and now!!"

Itsuwa vacillated a moment but eventually nodded.

She must have decided they didn't have time to waste summoning the members of Amakusa scattered around France.

In the meantime, hundreds of rioters were getting closer from the other side of the narrow road.

They looked packed in like sardines—a thick wall made of people.

"...When we go in, please stay low," said Itsuwa quietly as she stared at them. "If they see our faces in the middle of the pack, they could target us. But that's less likely if we can stay hidden in the crowds. Even if this riot is the enemy intercepting us, it doesn't look very precise."

"Right," said Kamijou, feeling something between fear and excitement. "Let's run!"

That moment, Kamijou and Itsuwa each plunged into the crowd of rioters.

They twisted and turned, wriggling through the riotous crowd as thick and dense as the walls that guarded the city. There were too many people to run. He could just barely walk and even then, only a few meters at a time.

Suddenly, with a shout, someone punched him in the head.

When he tried to keep going, large fingers grabbed his shirt.

From there on out, Kamijou was just as frantic as them. He bit an arm coming to grab him, pushed through the wall in his way, and went forward, albeit still dragging the hangers-on along behind. Blood crept from his side where nails had dug into him, and he caught the scent of excited men's body odor. Explosive yells right in his ear rattled his brain, and as the crushing pressure from every direction increased, his mind began to steadily wear down.

*Shit...*Little by little, his legs grew dull. *Shit...!!*

Just as the disgusting mass was about to swallow him whole, the wall of people suddenly parted. A breath of fresh air rushed in, untainted by all the human gasping.

"A-are you all right?!"

Itsuwa's voice came from right near him.

Blood was trickling from one of her temples. It didn't look like she could get through this crowd unharmed, either. She had mentioned a spear being in her bag, but she must not have felt like swinging it around.

Kamijou, heaving, ran to get out of the throng. Somehow, his feet felt wobbly and unreliable. If he wasn't being careful, he would have rammed a shoulder into the narrow road's stone wall.

"...I-Itsuwa, where's the palace?"

"Still up ahead. That roof all the way over there is it...W-we'll have to get past *that* next," she said, pointing.

Kamijou looked over slowly.

It was another human vortex, this one incomparably larger than the one they'd just struggled through.

5

The way to the Papal Palace was too perilous for them to make it through.

The old city of Avignon where Kamijou and Itsuwa were was a small one, spanning four kilometers and enclosed by stone walls, but they weren't making any progress toward their destination. The parts of the old city around them, at any rate, had tight roads. There were only about three meters from one side to the other, and on each side were housing complexes towering like ramparts, all made of stone as well. With the fifteen-meter-tall walls blocking them, it would be too hard to take a detour...and if they tried to plunge straight through, a riotous crowd of hundreds or even thousands would be waiting for them. When so many people crammed into such a narrow space, they formed a thick wall. It was like trying to walk from one end of a fully packed train car to the other.

They wouldn't get to their destination like this. The crowds seemed like they would do them in before they got to destroy the document.

"Again...," said Itsuwa, breathless, staring at the new mobs filling the space in front of them.

Kamijou didn't know French, but several of the men were shouting and pointing at the two of them, eyes bloodshot. Maybe they were calling out that the pair was from Japan or Academy City. Before the men could move, Itsuwa grabbed Kamijou's arm and started running.

"That...won't work. Please, come this way. Otherwise, we'll be trapped!"

"Hey, wait, what about the palace?" he shouted; Itsuwa had headed back down the road from which they'd come. The men staring at them before seemed to try and give chase, but they were immediately engulfed into the swirling riots.

Itsuwa, meanwhile, gritted her teeth, not happy with the situation, either. "...That mob is past critical numbers. We can't get through them by running!"

"You're going to use a different route? But..."

Kamijou was cut off by several young adults from a different riot showing up in their new escape route. The already tight path was now perfectly closed in by human walls.

Which made sense. Kamijou and Itsuwa had just gotten out of that one a few moments ago.

"Here too?!!" said Itsuwa, her voice unusually angry, pulling Kamijou's hand and running toward the housing complex walls. They burst inside one building, which looked like cliffs rather than stone-built structures. They shut the thick wooden door by ramming their backs into it.

Violent pounding and impacts recoiled through the door at them. It wasn't someone trying to bust down the door but rather the rioters' shoulders and arms scraping together.

Kamijou, his back resting against the door, slid down to the floor. "...What do we do now? We can't get anywhere near the Papal Palace like this."

"Yes, it does seem difficult to make any progress like this...," his companion replied weakly. She let her bag off her shoulder and onto the floor before taking seventy-centimeter rods out of it. When she clicked them together through gas stopcock-like sockets, they formed a single, long pole. Finally, she attached a steel blade to the tip.

Her Western cross lance was complete. He thought he remembered its name being a "Friulian spear," something used for shipboard combat.

He sighed. *Seems like she's rethinking the whole covert movement thing...Huh?!*

Suddenly, something caught in his throat as he thought.

He'd just gotten a glimpse of Itsuwa's cleavage through her blouse, which was only tied in the front. He thought to himself that her outfit was unfair in a few ways, but she didn't seem to notice whatsoever.

"What shall we do? I'd been operating under the assumption we would avoid the riots. I didn't actually prepare any plans or spells for if we actually got caught in them."

"W-well. We need to get to the palace to calm the riots, and we need to calm the riots to get to the palace...Damn, it just goes around in circles."

Not only that, but if the enemy felt like they were in a crisis, they could take the document home to the Vatican while they were stopped up like this. If they used it from there, taking it back would be very difficult. Then these contrived riots could just go on forever.

It was a dilemma—they needed to act swiftly, but they couldn't make a move.

Each second that went by wasted felt ten, even a hundred times longer.

And that was when it happened.

Suddenly, the cell phone in Kamijou's pocket played its ringtone.

It was from Tsuchimikado.

"Kammy, are you all right?!"

"Where the hell are you right now?! Wait, did you get caught in the riots, too? You'd better not be hurt!"

"I'm heading for a building called the Papal Palace right now. That's about the only place in France they can use the document from, nya."

"The Papal Palace...? You were going after that, too?"

"?"

Before Tsuchimikado could say anything, Kamijou added, "Which means my parachute didn't land me somewhere strange—we definitely had something to do in Avignon all along."

"Well, yeah, but...Kammy, how do you know about the palace? I thought we jumped from the plane before I could explain, nya."

"I met up with someone from Amakusa named Itsuwa, and she

told me something similar. But the riots got bad, and we can't get close. How are you doing?"

"About the same over here, nya. Well, some stuff *happened. Avignon's narrow streets go too well with these human wave riots. Can't even get near the place without busting straight through."*

With just that, each knew the other's general situation. Tsuchimikado must have also been caught in the riots and then withdrew somewhere.

"Hey, Tsuchimikado. I want to meet for now. Know anywhere we can join up?"

"There's riots happening all over the city. I'd like to avoid staying in one place for too long."

"Then what do we do? Wait for the riots to die down?"

"We could, if these were naturally occurring ones. *But this was all done intentionally with the document. Seeing that the Church can drag on this mess for as long as it's convenient for them, nothing will change for the better if we just wait around."*

"You have something else in mind?!"

"I do," answered Tsuchimikado simply. *"An idea to turn things around. If we can't go to the Papal Palace, we'll just have to solve the problem in a way where we don't need to."*

"...?"

"Did that Amakusa person tell you anything? No, so here's a question for you. Why are we so focused on Avignon's Papal Palace?"

Kamijou thought for a moment. "It's, uh, because they can remote control a building in the Vatican, right? That's how they can use the document from here."

"That's right. In that case, we just have to cut off the magical pipeline connecting Avignon and the Papal States...or the Vatican now. If we do that, they shouldn't be able to use it. Even if it's too hard to get to the palace, we might be able to reach a pipeline on the way."

"Oh!" blurted out Kamijou. He was right about that..."But if they can't use it, the guys trying to use it in the palace will realize, right? And then they might be able to get away."

"Yeah. Can't deny that. That's why everything rests on how we schedule this. It'll all come down to how fast we can get to the palace after severing the pipeline."

Tsuchimikado's plan seemed to make a certain amount of sense. Had he gotten that information before they'd boarded the plane? Or had he, after getting separated from Kamijou, been investigating Avignon while fleeing from the riots on his own?

Still, even Kamijou's amateur senses saw a problem with it. "If the document is in the Papal Palace, *we won't know who's using it, will we?* If they want, they could just blend into the crowds to hide. If that happens, it'll be really tough for us to find them on our own."

"..." On the other end of the line, the agent was quiet for a moment. *"Well, we'll manage it somehow. For now, stopping the document comes first."*

Kamijou didn't like where this was going...*Don't tell me he's gonna use sorcery to locate the enemy again.*

Motoharu Tsuchimikado had a handicap—when he used magic, it damaged him. But Kamijou knew he could ignore that handicap if he needed to. He'd been splotched with blood during the Daihasei Festival when they finally tracked down Oriana Thomson.

Aware of Kamijou's unease or not, Tsuchimikado's voice was cheerful. *"We finally have our way out, Kammy."*

6

Kamijou and Itsuwa passed through a housing complex and out a back door.

"Itsuwa, your friends...the Amakusa guys. They're still held up?"

"I...I'm sorry. We never thought this would happen. I sent an emergency message a few minutes ago, but they'd be lucky to get to us by tomorrow morning. If we were in Japan, we could have used one of the swirls for the Pilgrimage in Miniature movement spell..."

This road contained no blockades; it even started to seem like they could get to the Papal Palace without a problem. But they didn't know when another huge crowd would clog the streets again, so it was better not to waltz on through the long distance. They'd have to aim for the nearby pipeline, like Tsuchimikado had indicated.

"O-over here." Itsuwa, spear in hand, took the lead.

The "walls" on our sides are awfully tall. Taller than before..., he thought. This area looked like it had stone buildings built on top of cliffs that were already there. Even the black grime and dirt on the stronghold-like buildings made it seem like a kind of bulwark; he couldn't tell what the structures were for at a glance. The residential buildings, stores, and churches all had the appearance of fortresses.

"Um, I know the spot Mr. Tsuchimikado is referring to, but...is there really a pipeline connecting the Papal Palace to the Vatican there?"

"Don't ask me...," muttered Kamijou, looking toward his phone.

Tsuchimikado's voice came back buoyant. *"Well, different cultures read ley lines completely differently. There's not much doubt about this one, though."*

The "point" was apparently quite close to where Kamijou and Itsuwa were. They were fairly far from Tsuchimikado, so it had fallen to the two of them to cut the pipeline. "So, uh, what's this pipeline going to look like?" he asked. "It wouldn't, like...be sticking out of the ground, right?"

"Ley lines are basically flows of energy in the land. The energy could take any shape or direction. Even if a ley line has significance for one religion, it could mean nothing to another. That happens all the time. That's why I said different cultures read them differently..."

Kamijou still looked confused. Next to him, Itsuwa, possibly having picked up on the conversation from the phone's speaker, clarified, "It's like different ways to use ingredients."

In Western cuisine, things like Berkshire pork were high-class ingredients, but in Japanese cuisine—recent creative dishes aside—nobody took the slightest notice of it. In the same way, pulling out only the power you felt necessary from all the different kinds of energy seemed fundamental to using ley lines. Itsuwa had spoken smoothly and clearly about it, leading Kamijou to idly wonder if Amakusa specialized in spells using the lines.

"Anyway, there's no rank in these lands. Meaning we're the ones assigning our own value and using them, nya."

"An amateur wouldn't be able to tell just by seeing it, right?" asked Kamijou.

"Yep. An important Roman Orthodox ley line links Avignon with the Vatican. A distorted one, strictly speaking, that people created by destroying the geography," he continued smoothly. *"Ley lines shake easily. It's a basic concept in feng shui."*

"Right. I don't get what these ley lines are. But they'll be lines engraved right into the ground, right?"

"What I'm saying is that if someone levels the ground, they'll twist the ley lines there, too. Feng shui practitioners use things like the locations of mountains or directions of rivers to decide what spots are good or bad...but these days, it's not that uncommon for people to fill up rivers and shave away mountains."

"Sorcerers who make use of the land need to try hard, lest others develop over those important points," added Itsuwa.

...Sounds like a huge pain, Kamijou thought with a sigh.

"On the other hand, you can use sorcery calculations to change the geography, too. More precisely, it's closer to reselecting one ley line from many independent ones in a region, based on which flavors they can bring out the strongest. But if you mess up, you could ruin the balance and cause a huge disaster, so they end up being these huge national-scale projects, nya."

"Like the Church's pipeline...," muttered Kamijou.

"As I mentioned, there are so many lines throughout the land with heaps of different kinds of energy, you couldn't even count them all. Which, well, means it's extremely tough to pick out one line you're after without any hints," added Tsuchimikado. *"But if you have a search condition...in this case, a line tying the Papal Palace to the Vatican, it's a different story. You can find it just as easily as a car GPS can find a destination you give it, yeaaah~? Anyhow, if you two could go bust that pipeline soon, that would be great. Uh, Itsuwa, right?"*

"Y-yes!!"

"*Just want to confirm you knyow a spell or a way to destroy the pipeline.*"

"Um, well, I know an Amakusa-style one. It should cover anything standard, as long as it's Shinto, Buddhist, or Crossist..."

"*That should be all you need. If you find the pipeline on your end, you'll do it.*"

Kamijou quirked his head to the side as he listened to their exchange. "Wait, couldn't my right hand take out any of these ley lines or pipelines in one hit?"

He had a power called the Imagine Breaker. Whether sorcery or magic, a single blow would destroy any preternatural power.

Tsuchimikado, however, didn't approve of the suggestion. "*We don't know if your Imagine Breaker can actually destroy ley lines.*"

"Huh?" Kamijou asked, surprised. "But ley lines...they're magic... right? Then..."

"*About that,*" he interrupted. "*We don't really understand everything about your right hand. It can negate anything, magic or supernatural ability, but...for example...right. A person's 'life force' is an occult energy, but you can't kill people just by shaking their hands, can you?*"

"Well, no..."

"*I get the feeling there's some strange exceptions. And I think ley lines fall under that category. It's hard to imagine you touching the ground and the planet blowing up.*"

But at the same time, Misha Kreutzev hadn't tried to touch Kamijou's right hand, and Hyouka Kazakiri was unconsciously afraid of it.

"..."

Kamijou suddenly fell quiet and glanced at his hand.

...*Exceptions?*

How did it work on the inside? Did the way it worked mean something?

Thinking about it calmly, he realized he didn't know much about his own power, the Imagine Breaker. Part of it was because he'd lost his memories...but maybe he wouldn't know even if that hadn't happened. At the very least, there were no hints, much less answers, in the "knowledge" that remained after his amnesia.

In any case, severing that pipeline was their first priority now. Kamijou collected himself and looked ahead.

7

Kamijou and Itsuwa came to a small museum in Avignon.

The museum wasn't a big, isolated building. Like the other housing complexes and stores had been, it was just using a section of one of the fortresslike buildings towering to either side of the road. The small, ancient city of Avignon, surrounded by its ramparts, didn't have that much space to begin with. City planners had probably wanted to keep the scenery unified.

At the front entrance stood a signboard in French, but seeing as how the store's metal lattice shutter was pulled down over the wooden door, the plate near the doorknob probably had the word for *closed* on it. Even though today was a weekday afternoon.

"They probably closed up early for fear of the riots," said Itsuwa, looking up at the building.

Kamijou glanced at the sturdy shutter. "But according to Tsuchimikado, the invisible pipeline runs through this museum, right? How do we get in? Does Amakusa have some kind of lock-picking skill, or—?"

"Yah!" came a cute call, interrupting him.

A moment later, Itsuwa stuck her spear's tip through the gap between the shutter and the ground, then moved it, using something like the principle of leverage. The very cogs that moved the shutter creaked, then broke apart.

A high-pitched crime-prevention alarm went off, but Itsuwa ignored it as she pushed the shutter farther open and used the principle of leverage again to pry open the wooden door behind it. Then she waltzed inside.

"Come on, hurry."

"Um…Itsuwa?" said Kamijou, staring in shock at the girl. His eyes asked, *Weren't you supposed to be a normal girl...?* but she only looked at him blankly. Was she planning to punch out anyone who heard the clamor and came to the museum?

Fearful of the loud, shrill alarm, Kamijou entered as well. It wasn't well lit...Actually, it was pretty much pitch-black. They'd probably closed all the windows so the exhibits wouldn't get hit by direct sunlight. Their normal fluorescent lights wouldn't cause a problem, but right now, the only light was the faint glow of the emergency exit sign. Walking around in here made him uneasy.

"Tsuchimikado was saying..."

"Now that we're here, I can tell. Looks like it's over here."

Itsuwa went farther in, spear in hand. Kamijou followed; the floor was completely normal. Looking at where the glass exhibition showcases were, though, this one spot broke the rules for some reason. It was unnaturally empty.

Itsuwa looked slowly across the unnatural floor. After a few moments of observation, she eventually nodded, satisfied with something. "It definitely looks like it's here. I can feel power treated in Roman Orthodox fashion...a certain purification effect applied to other religions' spells. This ley line is unique to Western Crossist society. Though it's hidden quite well...I had to get fairly close before I could sense it."

Then she looked over at Kamijou. "...Mr. Tsuchimikado hasn't come yet, but we should do this before the enemy notices us. I'll get to work cutting the pipeline, so please stand back a bit."

"It doesn't look like there's anything there," said Kamijou, staring hard at the floor near Itsuwa. "...Is cutting it going to be that easy?"

"Well, breaking the ley line clean in two would take a lot more people." Itsuwa laughed. "We only need to make it so they can't use their Papal Palace–Vatican line. All I'm doing is damaging it a bit and shifting its direction slightly, so I can manage by myself."

"I see," he said, not really seeing.

Anyway, I can't let the Imagine Breaker get in the way. He backed up a few steps.

The Amakusa girl put down her bag and rummaged through it. She seemed to be choosing everyday items to use for the spell.

As he watched, he asked, "I forget—did Amakusa use stuff like that to make their spells?"

"Y-yes. Right now, I need...a camera, slippers, this pamphlet, a bottle of mineral water, white panties—"

After taking them out, Itsuwa gave a "hyaa?!" and hurried to put the article she'd probably just changed out of back into the bag. Her face grew bright red, but the rest of her froze completely.

"Wh-what's wrong, Itsuwa?"

"...Essential...," mumbled Itsuwa, still not moving. "It's absolutely essential for this spell..."

Her face drained of hope, she took the underwear back out with slow movements. Seeing her about to cry, Kamijou considered turning around, but she told him, "N-no, please don't worry about it"—so he couldn't move at all.

Meanwhile, she arranged the items from her bag on the floor. At first, it looked like a circle...but it was probably governed by some kind of minute regulations.

After she finished positioning them all, she spun the spear in her hand around and pointed its tip downward.

"Here I go," she said, a short declaration before taking it in both hands and stabbing it into the floor.

It hit the exact middle of the circle.

It didn't make the sound of a blade hitting stone.

The spearhead slowly vanished into the floor as though sinking into a swamp.

When Itsuwa cuts the pipeline, it'll make the document lose its effect. That means the riots happening in this old city should calm down, too, he said to himself as the girl kept her spear in the floor. It continued to sink deeper, ever so slowly.

But when that happens, the guys using the document in the Papal Palace will suspect they've failed. If they decide the prospects are grim, they could take it and run back to the Vatican.

Her foot moved—her heel kicked the floor.

The index fingers of her hands grasping the spear tapped out a rhythm on its handle.

It'll be a race against time. Once the riots are settled, we'll run to the Papal Palace right away. We'll coordinate with Tsuchimikado and capture them before they vanish from the building.

Over half the spear was now buried, and the end of the shaft had fallen to the height of her chest.

She took her hands off, then regripped the spear.

Then she bent her wrists and twisted it.

Like turning a giant key…

…the next thing to come was a sound.

However—

It didn't come from Itsuwa's spear.

Bam!!

Suddenly, some kind of attack ripped through the museum's outer wall and flew toward both the spear in the floor and Itsuwa.

In terms of what it felt like—a blade swung by a giant.

White in color.

The attack traveled a straight line toward Itsuwa.

When she realized it, she left the spear stuck in the floor and wheeled around behind it. The unleashed attack shot right past her, but the fragments of the destroyed wall—a big bundle of rocks—struck her spear directly.

"Itsuwa!!"

Upon receiving the attack, the spear bent in the middle like paper.

Itsuwa took the aftershock. Still grasping the broken spear, she bent over backward.

After stirring up a certain amount of destruction, the white attack swayed and vanished like smoke.

"Why, you…!!"

Itsuwa took each of the spear's broken halves in each hand. After removing the broken rod piece from the place where it was attached, she kicked the bag on the floor into the air, grabbed a replacement rod from out of it, and built the spear anew.

The second attack came a moment later.

Tearing through one outer wall after another, a white blade rushed in from outside the building at them.

The white blade's motion, having penetrated straight through from wall to wall, was erratic, like a child violently swinging a tree branch. But the overwhelming destructive force behind it changed things. Stone walls and flooring crumbled, glass showcases shattered, and all the fragments flew in every direction.

Boom-bang-crash!! A series of loud noises.

Kamijou, crouching, saw a thin powder dancing down.

Crap...This building won't hold up...!!

"Itsuwa!!" he shouted, gesturing for her to run to the exit.

She complied, and they hurried to the museum's front exit.

Meanwhile, white blades swung around and carved up the walls, hot on the heels of their prey.

It felt like with each strike, their aim was getting more precise.

Was the opponent getting used to how they were fleeing?

Or...

Was the attacker at a long distance, approaching little by little?

After barely scraping past a blade falling on them like a guillotine, they practically stumbled out of the museum.

And there...

"Well, well. As I thought, it seems this is less precise if I'm not at close range."

...they heard a voice from nearby.

Only a dozen centimeters or so in front of him...

Someone was there, as though they'd waited from the beginning, and now Kamijou was the surprised one.

The person in front of them didn't wait for him to answer before swinging his right arm.

Something white was coiling around it.

Despite the languid motion, it shot toward Kamijou's neck with the speed of a guillotine sliding down.

Boom!! came an air-splitting roar.

"Oooohhhhhhhh?!"

Kamijou immediately held his right hand out and it crashed into the white blade.

The blade blew to smithereens that very moment. And not metaphorically—it actually turned into a fine, white mist and burst out into their surroundings.

His attacker made a gesture with his fingers, and the roiling, fog-like curtain of powder reassembled.

"Please stand back!!" shouted Itsuwa from behind him.

Kamijou quickly put distance between them.

Finally, his eyes focused on the entire form of his assailant.

It was a man wearing a green dress uniform.

Perhaps short for a Caucasian, he was about Kamijou's height, if not shorter. On the other hand, he might have been twice Kamijou's age. He had a slender frame, and the uniform seemed to have some space on the inside. An odd sense of vitality exuded from his hollowed cheeks.

Kamijou kept his right hand up and asked the attacker in uniform, "...From the Church?"

"You aren't wrong, but I would have liked it if you'd called me God's Right Seat."

The man spoke with levity, and his words made Kamijou speechless.

God's Right Seat.

Once before, on September 30, Vento of the Front, one of their number, had almost completely paralyzed all of Academy City's functions by herself.

If he was on her level, then...

"My name is Terra of the Left."

The white powder, which had gathered at his hand, now took shape.

It was another guillotine.

A plank-shaped blade, as though cut apart diagonally from the lower part of a seventy-centimeter square. The man was grabbing it by the hole where the rope would normally hang from.

"It seems my turn has come at last. After all, we can't use the normal sorcery humans can—we must entrust the usage of the document to another caster."

Terra let the blade of execution dangle loosely at his side, speaking with a bemused tone.

And smile.

"And so, I'll have you accompany me to kill some time. You two are the first ones I've caught in the anti-ley-line investigation trap, so I'd very much appreciate it if you would let me have a little fun."

8

In front of the museum's destroyed outer walls were Kamijou, Itsuwa, and Terra. As the view worsened from the dust, they moved, splitting through it all.

Terra of the Left swung his right hand.

From left to right.

The white guillotine matched his hand's motion. He wasn't so much holding it as something floating in the air was moving in tune with his arm. The guillotine had been about a meter long, but now it abruptly lost its form, turned into a giant white wave, and mowed through everything in a horizontal sweep.

A rumbling *boom!!* split the air.

"Oooohhh?!" Kamijou instantly readied his right hand.

A moment later, the vortex of destruction shot after them. The streets of the old city of Avignon were narrow; the attack carved craters into the cliff-like buildings standing on either side, blew away cars parked on the road, and tilted the very buildings themselves.

Was it to Kamijou's right or his left? He didn't know—that was how neatly it was dividing the old streets and mountains of rubble.

The attack was certainly powerful, and he'd be helpless if it hit him straight on, but...

I can do something about that white blade with my right hand!!

"Itsuwa!!" he shouted, dashing off toward Terra without waiting for her to answer.

As he drew Terra's attack to him, Itsuwa used the time to slip closer. It was the most efficient pattern.

Meanwhile, Terra seemed to have taken notice of Kamijou's right hand.

Narrowing his sickly-looking eyes, he spoke with admiration. "Normally, you would have died from that attack just now. I see, so that is the Imagine Breaker…Still, I heard it nearly got the better of Vento of the Front."

With a smirk, he swung the guillotine.

From back to front.

To match the motion, the white blade sharpened, and the keen strike flew straight at Kamijou's chest.

"…!!"

He managed to block it with his right hand, but now that he had to focus on defense, his own movements dulled.

Whoosh!

Itsuwa ran by Kamijou's side in a low crouch, her spear at the ready.

"Hmph."

Terra directed his guillotine toward her.

A huge *boom!!* hit Kamijou's eardrums. The white blade had fired in a straight line, but Itsuwa had swung her upper body around to dodge it. Despite that, her feet kept moving. As she dodged a second critical attack, then a third, she regripped her Friulian spear and dove closer to Terra.

After pulling the spear back once, she unleashed a powerful forward thrust.

Terra repelled it with a sideways swipe of his guillotine. Then he moved it in the opposite direction, attacking Itsuwa from the side this time.

The giant blade shot out as a counterstrike.

"!!"

Itsuwa didn't force herself to parry it, instead jumping forward and to the side to evade while advancing. Meanwhile, she pulled her spear back and gave another full-force thrust with the energy.

But because of the extra dodge, Itsuwa lost her balance, and there was a moment before her attack began.

Terra used that moment to release the next guillotine.

At this rate, Terra's white blade would stab through her faster than her spear could hit him.

Flick.

A small light popped up next to Terra's face.

By the time it registered, rays of light had already crossed before her adversary's eyes, with many more of them winding and weaving through his surroundings like a spiderweb.

"Allow me to apologize..."

At the same time the words left the man's mouth, there was an alarming grinding sound.

Filled with her power, they were...

"...Seven Teachings, Seven Blades!!"

...steel wires.

A *ga-bam!!* split the air as the wires surrounding Terra blasted toward him. The superthin blades attacked him from seven directions, aiming to sever every part of his body, from his ankles to his heart.

Terra didn't have the time to get out of the way.

Kamijou thought they might have been traveling faster than bullets from a pistol.

However...

"...*Prioritize.*"

...Terra's expression didn't change.

All he did was mutter a single word. But the seven wires targeting his body didn't cut him up—in fact, they simply coiled around him like kite strings, not damaging his skin in the slightest.

Itsuwa's face filled with shock.

Terra lightly waved his right arm as if to split the spiderweb apart, ripping open the seven wires on his skin.

"!!" Itsuwa shoved her pulled-back spear forward. The sharpened head flew at lightning speed and nearly stabbed Terra through the shoulder.

"Prioritize—outer wall as low, human body as high."

It happened the moment Terra said those words. His body disappeared into the wall behind him, as if passing through an invisible hole.

"?!" Itsuwa's spear collided with the empty wall with a shrill *clang*. The impact traveled back up her wrists; she grimaced in pain. Then...

"Prioritize—outer wall as low, blade movement as high."

With a *whack!!*, the white guillotine pierced through the wall, then came in on a sideways sweep toward Itsuwa's torso.

She gave up on blocking, instead rolling onto the ground to evade the horizontal slash.

Strands of severed hair danced through the air.

Meanwhile, Terra reappeared outside from the gap in the outer wall he'd destroyed. Finding Itsuwa right after she'd taken evasive action, he recklessly swung the guillotine once again.

The girl, her body now pressed to the ground, couldn't avoid it.

So Kamijou jumped between them to interrupt.

"Wooohhhhaaaaahhhhh?!"

Just before the giant blade came down onto her neck, he sent it flying with his right hand.

The guillotine began to burst apart into a white powder.

Terra's expression remained level. Calm was the only thing on his face.

"Prioritize—outer wall as low, blade movement as high," declared Terra again, casually stabbing his reassembled white blade into the wall to his side.

Then he swung both the guillotine and the wall, as if knocking over shelves.

The outside wall fell apart, and ten or so rocks the size of melons came flying at him.

"!!"

Kamijou grabbed his champion's arm as she tried to get up and yanked her back. The spot they'd just been in immediately became buried in building materials.

Rather than chasing them right away, Terra walked slowly toward them, stepping on the rubble as he went.

"I heard about the Imagine Breaker before, and I must say, I was hoping for a bit more." Terra laughed in a low voice, his white blade of unknown composition hanging in his right hand. "As far as I can see, it doesn't seem like much. To be quite honest with you, I find myself disappointed at seeing it in real life. Disappointed enough to consider it not worth seeing. You apparently defeated Vento with it, because not only was her divine judgment gone but Academy City was also using things such as the fallen angel and the plane compression, strangling her from within. If her attacks had been at full strength, she would never have struggled against the likes of you."

Kamijou backed up as Terra moved forward, covering Itsuwa.

*This is...*Even as he felt a chill in his spine, somewhere in his mind, he was convinced. A man on Vento's level *would have more than just that blade to attack with.*

This is God's Right Seat...!!

He gritted his teeth, but Terra wasn't about to wait around for his confusion to settle.

"Oh my. What's the matter?" Terra laughed, ominous guillotine in hand. "I know you don't think backing up like that is enough to beat me. Please let me have some more fun. This won't help me tune it."

"Urgh!!"

Kamijou and Itsuwa, dragging their heavy bodies, charged at Terra at the same time.

Terra held his right hand with the guillotine in it out in front. "Prioritize—the spear movements as low, the air as high."

That was all it took for Itsuwa to grind to a sudden halt. The tip of her spear, which she'd flung out toward Terra's throat, stopped as if hitting a wall made of air.

Kamijou saw it out of the corner of his eye; he clenched his fist tightly and stepped toward Terra.

But the man was faster. A simple, casual sideways swing of the hand, and he fired the white blade. The giant blade grazed past Kamijou's right hand and stuck into his body.

Oh, shi—, he thought, before being cut off.

The blade, bigger than his thumb, pressed into his body. It felt like it was eating into him.

Pain exploded.

The guillotine continued, bending Kamijou in half, slamming him full force into the wall to the side.

Thwunk!! Then a painful snap from inside.

...?! The extreme situation disabled his ability to think.

Pressure jolted into his gut and his back at the same time, driving the air from his lungs.

"Gho...hah...?!"

But that was all.

Unlike the outside wall, it didn't cleave his body in two.

He took his trembling hand and punched the guillotine pinning him down. The giant blade exploded into a fine dust, and Kamijou fell to his knees, trying desperately to catch his breath.

"..." Terra stared at his destroyed guillotine with keen interest. He took a step back, flicked his fingers—and just like that, the powder returned to him.

I'm...alive? thought Kamijou, rubbing his stomach, which still throbbed. *A direct hit from that blade, and I'm alive...?*

Terra's very first attack had easily carved up the museum's outside wall. If he used the same attack, his body couldn't stand up to it.

Which meant...*That blade was different than the rest...?*

Kamijou looked from his stomach to Terra.

The man, standing in front of the ruined museum, was the picture of relaxation.

Is something amplifying its power? It must mean there's a trick to that blade.

One thing stood out as most suspicious.

Kamijou locked his eyes on Terra, who was checking the condition of his once-destroyed guillotine.

"Prioritize…," Itsuwa suddenly said, having pulled in her spear and swapped positions with Kamijou, now covering him. Then she noticed the powder stuck to the spear's tip. "…Flour?"

She thought for a moment, then her face lit up in surprise. "Wait, that weapon…It interacts with the body of Christ…?"

"Well, well. Even an Asian can tell?" said Terra, challenging the speechless Itsuwa. "During Mass, wine and bread are treated as the blood of Christ and the body of Christ. And for Mass itself, it's modeled, of course, after one thing—the crucifixion of the Son of God."

Itsuwa bit her lip. Kamijou didn't understand, but Terra's words seemed to pack a punch for people who knew magic.

"The Son of God was hung on the cross…but thinking rationally, it isn't normal for a regular human to be able to kill him. It would probably be hard even for me. But sometimes, in the legends, the order of priority changes. Like how a normal human killed him, ignoring the natural order, so that he could shoulder mankind's original sin."

His guillotine made a coarse sound as it crumbled. His expression was getting more and more amused, despite Kamijou being on his guard.

"The secret that completes the Son of God's legends…*Changing the order of priority*. That is the true form of my only spell, Light's Execution. The optional transformation into a blade with flour as the medium is like a side effect. I wonder—do you understand now?"

In other words, this is what he meant: Terra had prioritized his body over the wires, so he hadn't been wounded. He'd prioritized the blade made of flour over the outside wall, which gave it all that destructive potential. He'd prioritized the air over the spear, which stopped Itsuwa's attack dead in its tracks.

"Strength and weakness mean nothing before me," said Terra. "Because I can control their very order."

This was the power of God's Right Seat.

Vento of the Front had attacked Academy City's functions wielding her divine judgment, used by gods. This time, it was the Son of God's crucifixion.

Every sorcerer Kamijou had ever met used queer theories and rules that he didn't know anything about, but he got the feeling the ones God's Right Seat used were unique.

"But what shall happen now? I've revealed the secret, *but now what?* I'm sure you don't think everything's over now that the mystery is solved."

Kamijou unconsciously tightened his right fist at Terra's words.

He was right. Just because he knew how it worked didn't mean he could find a way to beat it. That was why Terra had so calmly revealed his trick to them.

"Why don't I give you some time?" said Terra mockingly. "For me, drawing this battle out isn't terribly bad. I'll give you ten seconds. Please come up with a plan in that time, whether it's to defeat me or flee…if such a thing exists, of course," he said, amused, or perhaps searching.

"Shit," spat Kamijou despite himself. Was the gap between him and Terra of the Left that big?

As Kamijou clenched his teeth, Terra watched, as if to savor each of his reactions…

"Real nice of you. With ten seconds, I could think of three plans."

…when suddenly, Kamijou heard a familiar man's voice come from the side.

Before he could look over, a red bullet pierced through the air. It was a piece of origami, wrapped in an orange flame. The complex folds in the square paper shot toward Terra's face with the strength to tear apart concrete.

All Terra did was move his eyes in that direction. "Prioritize— sorcery as low, human skin as high."

It was a direct hit. But the moment the origami touched Terra's skin, it radically changed direction and crashed into the wall right next to Itsuwa. The response was like a bullet ricocheting off a metal wall.

Kamijou finally looked at the intruder.

Standing there was a boy wearing blue sunglasses.

As a side effect of forcing the sorcery, a bead of blood trickled from his lips.

"Tsuchimikado…?!"

The youth nodded slightly in response. His eyes were still on Terra.

"Really, now." Terra chuckled, right hand holding the dangling guillotine. "I do hope that wasn't your plan to overcome the situation."

"Unfortunately, no."

Tsuchimikado was smiling as well. Despite his attack ending in failure, only calm filled his expression.

"That was to back you into a corner."

"…?"

"My next move will be checkmate. What I'm saying is that my deductions are being confirmed."

As he spoke, he took something out—something not related to magic.

It was a shining black handgun.

The same one he'd used to shoot Monaka Oyafune in the stomach.

"You think a toy like that could beat me?"

Tsuchimikado didn't answer. He squeezed the index finger on the trigger.

Standing in the road without any particular cover to hide behind, Terra slowly opened his mouth.

""Prioritize—bullet as low, human skin as high.""

Tsuchimikado's voice overlapped Terra's.

Bang-bang-bang!! A series of gunshots.

The lead bullets struck Terra's face and heart but then bounced off.

The result was clear.

Despite that, the smile on Tsuchimikado's lips didn't disappear.

"Terra of the Left…"

Keeping the gun level with one hand, his other dove into his pocket.

He took out a black piece of origami.

"I told you it would be checkmate."

"…"

Terra stayed quiet.

Then, slowly, he readied his guillotine again.

An odd silence overtook the streets, which should have been wrapped up in rioting.

It's changing…, thought Kamijou.

For better or worse, the battle situation was about to change significantly.

He almost found himself absorbed by their confrontation, but then Itsuwa, who had approached without him realizing, whispered into his ear:

"(…Um, when Mr. Tsuchimikado moves, I'll take advantage and run in.)"

"Huh?"

"(…I have a message from him. Defeating him isn't important— stopping the document in the Papal Palace is.)"

Itsuwa showed him a piece of origami in her hands.

It must have had directions from Tsuchimikado on it. He didn't know when he'd given it to her, but he'd probably flung it at her while talking to Terra.

Tsuchimikado and Terra both inched forward, step by step.

They were about to clash.

Right as Kamijou thought that, there was a roaring noise loud enough to pierce his eardrums.

…?!

It wasn't caused by sorcery.

It was the sound of a bomb demolishing the streets of Avignon.

Obviously, it wasn't something Tsuchimikado or Terra had caused.

A third party had interrupted.

As proof, both of them swore and retreated a distance.

As Kamijou looked on in surprise at the sudden event, the outside walls of the housing complexes towering over the roadside like cliffs began to crumble. A gray dust cloud whipped up and began to block their vision.

On the other side of it, he saw the silhouettes of the things that caused the explosion.

But they were very far from being human.

"...What the hell? What's going on here?"

Where Kamijou looked, hidden beyond the curtain of gray, distorted human shapes crawled.

9

Academy City's unofficial composite armored unit began the attack on the old city of Avignon from its edges.

Their main armament was the HsPS-15, code-named "Large Weapon"—a powered exoskeleton suit built with the very best technology Academy City had to offer.

Powered suits were Academy City's new weapon. Covered in special armor resembling Western plate mail, they used electrical power to move their joints and granted dozens of times the strength of a regular human being.

Different standards specified different sizes and combat capability, but each here was a hunk of metal with a total height of two and a half meters.

These machines, specially camouflaged in blue and gray, each had robot-like armor with two arms, two legs, and even five fingers on each hand. But if one were to ask if these powered suits looked human, the answer would be no. Their headpieces were enormous, and when added to their large chest armor, it made it look like they were wearing oil-drum-shaped police robots on their heads. They had no neck; their headpieces rotated on a fixed axis atop the chest.

Snap-snap-snap-snap!! The sound of hard objects being crushed. It was the noise from their legs trampling over rubble.

They were destroying the wreckage of the stone and brick streets, which had lasted hundreds of years with incredible ease.

The powered suits gripped special firearms, their barrels awkwardly thick, in their hands. They looked like large rifles—like tank cannons cut short—but strictly speaking, that was incorrect.

They were anti-bulkhead revolver shotguns.

The ammunition these firearms used was special. Dozens of bullets that would be loosely classified as anti-matériel were crammed into each shell; every single shot packed enough punch to blow through a tank. A few shots from short range could even wrench open the door to a nuclear shelter. Normally, the barrel wouldn't be able to withstand the gunpowder's explosiveness, but through fine adjustments to the type of powder and loading position, the gun delivered the most destructive potential for the least possible strain on the weapon.

These armaments were developed for breaking down and devastating thick shelter entrances, which enemies often holed up behind. Now, dozens of powered suits had these guns trained on Avignon's ramparts.

"Commence invasion."

Two short words.

As the voice spoke, flames erupted from their anti-bulkhead shotguns. Each time they pulled the slide, like a pump-action rifle the revolver's cylinder rotated.

The stone walls, which had restricted entrance for centuries, blew away like tissue paper in the wind.

The powered suits stepped over the wreckage and began to enter the old city of Avignon.

Their artificial limbs advanced more smoothly than real humans could have.

In front of them were the young people who had been rampaging through the city. They showed no single emotion like fear or anger; instead, the abruptness of the situation tossed them into a mixed-up vortex of emotion that defied any such easy classification. Even their bones were rattling.

Meanwhile, the powered suits' response was incredibly simple.

They aimed their thick shotgun muzzles, which had blown apart the ramparts in one shot, straight at the humans.

A curt voice spoke to his allies over the radio.

"Enemy faction spotted."

10

Upon seeing the swarm of powered suits ignoring the tightly interlocking roads of Avignon and breaking down whatever walls they wanted to walk where they pleased, Kamijou was stunned. The walls of the cliff-like buildings towering over them broke down, and on the other side of the wreckage was *them*.

Such things weren't supposed to exist in the normal world.

Academy City was likely the only facility that could develop powered suits of a practical level.

In their hands, they held anti-bulkhead revolver shotguns.

As they blew through one obstacle to their advance after another, tearing through buildings and cars, they also began mercilessly pointing their muzzles at the recklessly counterattacking rioters.

Flame burst from a gun barrel that was easily thick enough to fit one's fist into.

With echoing crashes and bangs, it mowed down swaths of people effortlessly.

But those probably weren't real bullets. Kamijou didn't know how they operated, but the anti-bulkhead shotguns were probably made to use different bullets for different purposes. Maybe the gun distinguished how to handle them on the inside of the revolver's cylinder, based on whether it was an even shot or an odd shot, rotating two shots at a time. If that was the system, then switching modes between even and odd would sort of make sense.

They were firing blanks.

However, the shock waves, which used a ton of explosives to fire, was all it took to drive the oxygen from the people's lungs and send their bodies careening to the ground. Once they silenced the first wave of hot-blooded rioters, the ones standing back as the second and third waves went white-faced and began running every which way.

The powered suits didn't overlook them.

After passing by a civilian who was cowering in the street and trembling, they fired blanks without mercy at anyone who showed even the slightest sign of resistance. The sound of shells kept on clapping. Then when the force had neutralized the immediate rioters, they affixed their shotguns to their metal backpacks, leaving the machines to automatically reload them.

...What's going on? Kamijou could do nothing but stare at the absurd situation. *Didn't Tsuchimikado say Academy City wasn't going to do anything? And even if they decided to, why the hell are they going about it so senselessly?!*

Monaka Oyafune had talked about Academy City's higher-ups purposely not making a move, thus trying to make the current chaos worse.

Did this mean the time was ripe?

Were they trying to end it all with a flip of the switch since the damage from the chaos had exceeded what was deemed allowable?

Kamijou clenched his teeth.

Academy City's higher-ups.

The General Board.

And the true top of the science side who led them.

"I see. It's come to that, has it?" said Terra, sounding amused.

With those few words, he retook control of the air colored by shock around them.

Even Tsuchimikado, leveling his smoking gun muzzle, was emitting a piercing enmity.

"As the ones using the document in the Papal Palace are, indeed, normal casters, this looks to be something of a predicament," said Terra. "I had wanted to collect more combat data for my priority spell, Light's Execution. Ah, well."

Without sparing a glance for any of them, Terra rolled into a housing complex whose outer wall was blown open by a powered suit and left.

"Wait!!" shouted Tsuchimikado, but a split second later, he jumped to the side.

Before Kamijou realized why, a huge blast exploded from inside the complex—possibly coming from a powered suit.

With the thundering *boom!!* Kamijou's tiny body was swept off his feet and thrown backward. The gaping hole Terra had gone through was instantly covered in flames.

"Ow...?!"

"Are...are you all right?!" cried Itsuwa, hurrying to take his hand.

As she helped him up, Tsuchimikado shouted, "Kammy, can you move? We're going for the Papal Palace, too!!"

"Those powered suits have got to be from Academy City!! I thought they weren't supposed to move!! They're just making things worse. Shouldn't we be stopping them?!" Kamijou shouted.

"Following Terra comes first!! And they're after the document, too. We might be able to calm the chaos by destroying that Soul Arm!!"

"Damn it," he spat bitterly. "That better be what they're really after—calming the chaos."

The document riots and the powered suits—which were the people of Avignon really more afraid of?

"Let's go, Kammy. God's Right Seat has made light of us in the past. But now that things are like this, they'll try to escape with seriousness. Now's our only chance to destroy the document!!"

"Shit," he cursed reflexively.

Several powered suits clambered out of the flaming hole in the wall Terra had escaped through and were now out onto the narrow road.

They aimed straight for them, even though they were Academy City citizens, too.

It didn't seem like they'd bother to ask who they were with. They'd set every single person in Avignon as an attack target.

"...Kammy, let's split into two. Itsuwa, right? You take Kammy and head for the Papal Palace."

"Tsuchimikado?" Kamijou asked, confused.

"It looks like Avignon has two problems now. I thought we could leave the powered suits to their own devices, but that's not looking hopeful. Kammy, follow Terra and do something about the document. I'll stop these party-crashing Academy City idiots."

"But you—" *can't do that*, he tried to say, before Tsuchimikado interrupted.

"They're not completely hostile. We'll fight for now, but I'll basically be looking for a chance to talk to them. I think I'm a little more cut out for a gamble like that than you, Kammy."

"...Damn it."

"Kammy, go!!"

"Damn it!!" shouted Kamijou, running with Itsuwa down the slender street. From behind, they heard the noises of the powered suits moving and—Tsuchimikado must have done something—a series of what sounded like ice shattering. Kamijou clenched his teeth. He knew using sorcery just once would leave Tsuchimikado bloody, but there was nothing he could say to him.

They ran down the narrow path and advanced through the old city of Avignon.

He smelled gunpowder and smoke.

Saw frantic people escaping and powered suits chasing them with surgical precision.

What the hell is going on?!!

This wasn't even comparable to the demonstrations and riots. The sight of this overwhelming violence called "military action" made Kamijou feel like he was about to burst a blood vessel.

Itsuwa, who had already been investigating Avignon, remembered where their goal, the Papal Palace, was. As she ran ahead to guide him, he looked up and saw its outline ahead.

INTERLUDE
THREE

Stiyl Magnus had briefly left the Tower of London.

The city was seeing fairly sunny skies today, but tourists were sparse. Unlike other nations, England hadn't experienced any large-scale rioting, but that didn't keep an air of tension from spreading through the streets.

"God's Right Seat, eh...?" Stiyl said to himself, a freshly lit cigarette in his mouth.

According to Lidvia Lorenzetti, it only had four official members, but each possessed the attribute of one of the four archangels.

"What do you think of their story?" said Agnes Sanctis in a bored tone, having left the building with him. "I wonder how much of it's true. At least, I know I've never heard anything about such matters when I was with the Church. They could be feeding us lies to throw us off their scent."

"I can't deny that, but anything said in those interrogation rooms is magically recorded. The things you wrote on that parchment, if we analyze it, we'll be able to tell the truth from the lies."

"Can't say it'll be perfect, of course," added Stiyl, thinking to himself. If Lidvia was telling the truth, God's Right Seat referred to both an organization in the dark side of the Church and to their ultimate goal.

...The seat on the right. Sounds like a hint, but it might not be. It isn't enough to narrow things down. For now, I suppose I'll see what else they have to say.

Stiyl glanced over at Agnes. "Should we take a break for a little longer?"

"No, let's get this finished up already."

"All right."

They returned to the dark Tower of Execution.

CHAPTER 4

Steel Swarm Covering the Sky
Cruel_Troopers.

1

Kamijou ran through the streets of Avignon.

Despite all their earlier terror, the rioters were no more. Most of them had been exterminated.

With overturned chunks of pavement and broken buildings' stones all over, the roads were in no condition for them to advance normally.

A slew of cars were sitting around, too. Kamijou burst through the smoke and gunpowder-corrupted air, running through holes in walls and scaling the occasional piece of rubble on his way to the Papal Palace.

Powered suits were swarming the streets. Some on the road, others on the tops of buildings. If a quick glance showed this many of them, there must have been hundreds, even *thousands* of them in all of Avignon.

Damn it. What's going on here...? he wondered, running through roads that had been flooded from burst water pipes while being careful to avoid fallen streetlights. *The Church set up this war, right? Academy City should be trying to stop that. How the hell did it turn out like this?!*

Something important was missing in this battlefield.

The smell of blood.

The powered suits' anti-bulkhead revolver shotguns seemed capable of using different bullets for different purposes; blanks were the only things hitting live people. The colossal amount of explosives they used, though, made those shots into shock waves, and their sonic shells were mercilessly mowing down Avignon residents.

Here and there were hills made of unconscious demonstrators. Just nearby were exoskeletons, inflating giant balloons with bulletproof fibers woven into them.

For reconnaissance...? He'd seen something like this in an Academy City–made drama.

They were loaded with small cameras and moved through the sky by warming the air—like hot-air balloons. Their shortcoming was their extreme battery consumption due to the electronic reactors they used to heat the air. Still, they were quieter than propellers. Above all, each unit was cheap and well suited to carrying around.

The balloons that the powered suits were inflating now were many times larger than the ones in dramas. These even had gondolas on them, with the same bulletproof fibers as the balloons' bottoms.

They were probably used in a similar way as regular hot-air balloons. Essentially, they were to toss unconscious people in while leaving it to the floating machines to eject them from the battlefield.

He glanced around again, finding the black balloons floating all over the sky like dandelion fluff adrift in the wind.

That view was, ultimately, how many people the powered suits had mowed down.

"..."

Perhaps they were thinking the same as Tsuchimikado.

The rioters strutting through the confined Avignon were making the mission difficult. The enemy with the document could have also been blending into those riots to flee. Therefore, they would first quell the riots, then get to work on their main objective.

However...

"Tsuchimikado wouldn't have done it this way…"

"Huh?" Itsuwa turned her head toward him, but Kamijou didn't answer.

As he ran, he balled his hands into tight fists, looking at the exploded cars. *Putting their own actions above everyone else, using violence to force the people in the streets to submit…He'd never accept this kind of method!!*

Finally, Kamijou realized what one of the General Board, Monaka Oyafune, had wanted to stop. She didn't simply hate the Roman Orthodox Church. She didn't want him to defeat Academy City's enemies, either. Everything had been about wanting to prevent this situation—this all-destroying "conflict."

I'll stop it. Kamijou clenched his teeth and ran through the town-turned-battlefield. *There's no way we can leave this destructive vortex alone. If someone shows up and tries to justify this situation even a little, I'll smash their illusion to smithereens!!*

"W-we're here. It's right over there…!!"

In the meantime, Kamijou and Itsuwa arrived at the Papal Palace.

From the name, he'd imagined a magnificent church or a glittering palace, but what actually stood before them was a stronghold from the Middle Ages—more a fortress than a castle. The giant building, constructed with multitudes of quarried rocks and boulders, even seemed to make those who witnessed it feel rejected.

The moment he saw the Papal Palace standing proudly and looking down at him with an outer wall over ten meters tall, Kamijou scowled.

"A crack…," mumbled Itsuwa, carrying her spear.

The giant double-doored front entrance had been blown out from inside, and the windows on high floors had been smashed up along with the walls nearby. He started hearing sporadic gunshots and the sounds of explosions.

"Damn, it's already started. Let's go, Itsuwa!!"

"R-right!!"

Going into a building noisy with gunshots was far from a normal thought to have, but they had no choice.

2

Motoharu Tsuchimikado had blood on him.

It wasn't from being shot by powered suits; rather, it was a side effect of using his origami sorcery to divert their attention.

But now he had a chance, incredibly slim though it may have been, as he ran down the narrow, winding road before rolling behind a parked car.

Several reports screeched through the air toward him.

Those blanks were strong enough to suppress insurgents, even though they were nothing but masses of air. In one volley they shattered the car's glass, sonic masses pounding on its metal doors and instantly denting them.

You've gotta be kidding me... Tsuchimikado tsked, still clinging fast to the side of the car. He wouldn't easily die if one hit him but getting knocked out was a foregone conclusion. Now motionless behind his shield, Tsuchimikado suddenly heard a dull *bang!!*

Surprised, he whipped his head around—just as one of the several powered suits that had been pursuing him bounded over ten meters through the air with shocking power and readied itself straight above him.

"Shit!!" Tsuchimikado immediately retreated, just as the suit's massive bulk crushed the car underfoot. Unable to stand the weight, the vehicle crumpled and exploded all at once. Tsuchimikado took the shock wave and was sent careening farther than his own jump.

As he bounced and rolled onto the road, the powered suit in the flames calmly aimed its gigantic shotgun muzzle at him.

He was in an area with cliff-like buildings lined up on either side of a tight road. He tried to swing around a corner to use a building as a shield, but the powered suit moved before he could. A mass of air fired with a crack, landing a hit on his leg.

The leg sweep sent him tumbling.

As he lay on the ground, he managed to round the bend.

Guh...ahhhhhh?!

He looked around his ankle and saw it change to a bluish black. His bone seemed to have managed to remain unbroken, but he made no mistake: It would limit his movements.

As far as I can tell, there are...fourteen powered suits. Their armor looks thin, but they'd be able to take an anti-tank missile head-on. Plus...

As he listened to the mechanical operations from around the corner, Tsuchimikado took out emergency tape from his pocket and tied it firmly around his ankle.

...they're using the new drive compensators. They'll learn from the battlefield conditions and adjust themselves to give the most efficient performance.

Using such weapons would be more or less effective given the environment, such as a tropical rain forest or Antarctica. In a desert, sand getting in would require care, and in wetlands, one would need to make sure mud didn't get caught up in it.

Most machines were maintained to be easy to use in specific environments, their weapons' features naturally changing with the region, but these powered suits were different. These machines would scan the nearby environment and automatically adapt themselves to it, allowing them to perform well at default settings in battlefields throughout the world.

And they'll be exchanging their auto-adjust info to every unit in the operation. Ha-ha...They'll probably know how to traverse Avignon better than the locals.

Maintaining balance was the bottleneck for legged weapons, but Tsuchimikado wouldn't be able to use that weakness against them. Even if the ground under them was falling apart, they'd walk more skillfully than a human and overcome it.

Damn. How do I attack...? He muttered to himself as he double-checked the tape on his ankle.

And all the while, they were approaching.

3

The Papal Palace's interior was spacious.

But it had a loneliness to it, Kamijou thought. There were no things here. Not even wallpaper—the stone walls surrounding them stood bare. Other than the evenly spaced pillars supporting the ceiling, nothing was in here. It was like a pyramid after someone had run off with all the treasure.

Like we thought...It doesn't look like the Church stationed a major force in Avignon. If they're only using a small elite team, does that mean they want to hide the document from the rest of the Church, too? Terra might even be the only one on the team.

"It...doesn't look like anyone is here," said Itsuwa, holding her spear at the ready. This place was open to the public on weekdays for tourists, but that was out of the question right now. Avignon had been scared of the rioters' shadows until now, and the building was the center point of the rampaging powered suits.

The gunshots and explosions continued even now.

If they were continuing, then was there an actual battle happening rather than just a one-sided subjugation?

Other sorcerers besides Terra seemed to be here in Avignon to use the Document of Constantine. Academy City's powered suits were one thing, but the Church was another. They couldn't afford for both factions to attack them here and now.

However, Kamijou's pace had slowed. "...Those powered suits... Where did they come from anyway?"

"Huh?" Itsuwa looked at him.

"Are there Academy City people piloting those, or did they lend them to some group?" he continued. "Besides, they can't possibly hide them after standing out this much. What the heck is Academy City planning to do...?"

His cell phone had a television function. Making any careless noises in this situation was dangerous, but he decided he wanted information more.

After making sure nobody was around, Kamijou got his cell phone out and turned on its television, but it didn't show anything, probably because it didn't work with overseas stations. He thought for a moment, then brought up his saved numbers list. He chose one and called it.

"Misaka!!"

"*Wh-what?*"

He was calling Mikoto Misaka.

"I wanted to ask you something. Do you have time right now?"

"*R-really, now. It has to be me, does it? You can't ask someone else? My mother, for example?*"

"Huh? …Oh, right, I guess so. I could just ask Ms. Misuzu instead of you."

"*Non, non, non, non, non!! H-hold on—didn't you call me because you wanted to ask* me *something?*"

"??? Well, I suppose you'd be better than Ms. Misuzu since you live in Academy City." Kamijou was a little confused but got to the point. "Can you turn on the news? Or the Internet. I want you to check foreign news to see if something's happening in a city called Avignon."

"*What?*" muttered Mikoto, probably because the question was so sudden.

…That was what he thought anyway. Apparently, the reality was different.

"*What the heck are you talking about? There's news flashes going on every television in the city. Avignon is that city in France, right? They're talking about how some religious group made special weapons of destruction against international laws and started trying to gain total control of the place.*"

"…What?" said Kamijou, startled.

"*Seems like the French government would normally settle this, but they needed experts in special technology, so Academy City is pretty deeply involved…Wait, where are you anyway? I'd think it would be harder to find a place where you* didn't *get this information.*"

"Um, well, that is…," stammered Kamijou, wondering how to fool her, but his thoughts were interrupted.

The roaring had ceased.

The sounds of battle, mostly gunshots, had suddenly stopped without him realizing it. The painful silence of the Papal Palace's normative state was slowly returning.

…

Mikoto said something on the other end. Kamijou didn't answer her. He held his breath and listened, but he still didn't hear anything at all.

He exchanged glances with Itsuwa and slowly walked forward.

What is this…?

He felt an indescribable sense of tension seeping to him from down the passage, from between the walls, from past the doors. It was like the very air around them was being remade into something other than what was already here.

Kamijou couldn't penetrate the cause.

Because before he could, the answer came from the other side.

Wsshhwwsshh!!

With a roar, the thick wall right next to Kamijou suddenly broke.

The identity of what had crashed through the wall was quickly found to be a powered suit. It rammed into Kamijou, instantly knocking him to the floor. The cell phone in his hand clattered away, its liquid crystal display smashed to bits.

"Urgh?!"

Itsuwa hastily thrust her spear's head toward the attacker, but her hands stopped halfway.

The powered suit's limbs were hanging limp, driven to a state of dysfunction. Someone had thrown it—that seemed the most apt way to describe it.

Cylindrical objects were scattered around where it landed—juice can–like cylinders, 350 millimeters wide. Were they the shells for the suit's anti-bulkhead shotgun? A giant revolver that looked like their source was lying nearby.

"Ugh..." Kamijou stood up and shook his head, then heard the *ka-click* of a footstep.

He looked up.

Itsuwa had her spear up, standing before him as a guard.

Past her...

...on the other side of the wall, broken down by sheer force, was a sorcerer holding a giant white blade.

Terra of the Left.

The man who had just used his prioritize spell to destroy the powered suit didn't have a bead of sweat on him.

"You certainly got me good," he said in a slow, relaxed tone with just a hint of irritation mixed in. "To stop the chaos of the riots, they caused an even greater chaos to swallow it up. I suppose Academy City is quite serious about this in their own right. They must want to deal with *this little thing* even if it draws a certain amount of international criticism."

His left hand, opposite the one holding the white guillotine...

...gripped a rolled-up piece of parchment. A small paper, condensed to about fifteen centimeters long and three centimeters in diameter. Sealed with wax, it was none other than...

"The Document of Constantine...," breathed Itsuwa, amazed.

The Soul Arm was mighty enough to make someone believe anything the speaker said was completely correct in Roman Orthodoxy. If Terra had it, rather than the original caster using it, that meant...

"I say, they are quite the bothersome lot. I could easily rout them all myself, but when they focused their attacks on the caster using this, it affects even my spell usage. I swear, my body's makeup is such a problem, what with it unable to use human techniques. Average spellcasters ended up holding me back because of it...so I suppose calling it quits here would be for the best."

"You think I'll stay quiet and let you go?" demanded Kamijou, slowly readying his right hand. "You can use the document even after you go back to the Vatican. You know that, and you still think I'll let you go?"

"But what's the point? Even the forces of Academy City suppressing Avignon here cannot stop me. Do you mean to say your right hand surpasses them all? Have you any proof for such a declaration?"

"..." Now that the gunshots in the Papal Palace had ceased, it was best to think Terra had defeated all the powered suits attacking it.

Boasting that much true power, the man laughed, further scorning Kamijou and Itsuwa. "Still, I suppose it would be difficult to convince you while doing nothing," he said, putting away the document in his left hand and calmly taking up the white guillotine in his right.

"Please fight to your heart's content and resign to your heart's content. I do so love it when things are interesting."

4

The Avignon townscape was coming down, piece by piece.

With blanks like shock waves, the knocked-out rioters were being dragged away by sturdy powered suits, piled up into mountains, thrown into balloons woven with bulletproof fibers, and then sent off to who knew where.

In the midst of it all ran Motoharu Tsuchimikado.

Changing from one position to another, from behind rubble to behind cars, he continued his flight from the powered suits pursuing him by making minute changes to his movement. Despite making a myriad of course corrections to put himself behind as many obstacles as possible, bursts of gun discharges were still intermittent. He had to avoid flat ground as much as possible, choosing places with fallen streetlights or ruined roads to advance, but...

Shit. This isn't enough to trip them up. Those drive compensators are really working...!!

Regardless of being unbalanced bipedal creations, and despite their considerable weight, the powered suits didn't seem harried in their movements in the slightest. This wasn't the kind of walking they'd done on flat ground, with each step a destructive stomp, but rather smooth, cockroach-like movements.

These powered suits would scan and automatically optimize for every environment and circumstance. They advanced as fast as cars and tread across the ground more lithely than the average human as they chased Tsuchimikado.

Checkmate would only be a matter of time.

Tsuchimikado stopped in the middle of the road. The tall buildings to his left and right were in tatters, blocking it off like a landslide. The rubble was fairly large. He'd be able to get over it if he grabbed the fragmented bumps and climbed, but the powered suits wouldn't give him that kind of time. They'd shoot him in the back as he clung to it, and that would be the end.

The *ka-click* of metal sounded behind him.

A dull sound like gears turning.

A chill crawled up Tsuchimikado's spine. He hadn't heard this sound yet—the sound of something switching. It was easy to imagine what had caused it.

…The anti-bulkhead shotguns.

It was the sound of them switching from their riot-suppression blanks to the real bullets, the kind that could break down nuclear shelter gates.

Here it comes!! Without turning around, he jumped to the side with all his might. A moment later, the burst of an explosion hit his body. The landslide of rubble blocking the way forward vanished into thin air with a roar. That single shot had opened up a circular hole meters wide.

"…!!" Covering his ears, Tsuchimikado glanced behind him.

The powered suit aiming its fist-sized barrel at him put its finger to the trigger again.

Avignon's roads were narrow.

It was impossible to jump to the side any farther to dodge.

"?! Hey, wood-for-brains, you can at least serve me as shields!! *Use the green tree talisman and protect my body!!*"

The same moment Tsuchimikado took out a piece of origami and shouted, the gunshot roared from right in front of him.

With a thunderous *bang!!,* dozens of anti-matter shots burst forth—only to bounce off the tiny shield in front of Tsuchimikado. They scattered, destroyed the surrounding buildings' walls.

A chunk of blood spurted from his lips.

The side effect of sorcery.

Nevertheless, he took out another piece of origami, black this time, and shouted.

"Wake up, you shitheads. Bust up everything so we can go home laughing!! *The color black is the symbol of water. Use its violence and open the path!!"*

A watery orb about one meter across suddenly appeared out of thin air. It shot into the powered suit, sending the machine flying backward all at once.

But that was the limit.

Tsuchimikado's side was slowly leaking blood now from using sorcery in succession. He tried to put his hand on what remained of an old building, but his legs gave out from underneath before it reached.

"Damn…"

A quick glance around revealed several exoskeletons. Others were aiming at him from building tops, too.

…As Tsuchimikado checked where each of them was located, he slowly raised his hands. He moved his lips and produced the words: "I surrender…Do with me what you wish.

"That is," he added, "if you can."

The instant he said that, a change occurred in the powered suit that held its barrel toward him.

Ga-clunk.

The powered suits, which had been moving more fluidly than normal humans, had suddenly tensed up. They quickly began to do an actions check, but they simply creaked and groaned as though their gears had clogged. They couldn't move a finger, so he would hear no gunshots.

"You want to know?"

He slowly approached and communicated with them.

They may have been powerful weapons, but people like him were controlling them.

"You've got those new drive compensators in those things. Whether you're in a desert or Antarctica, the machines will automatically investigate the environment and do their own maintenance for you.

"But," he said, "that can end up tying you down in certain cases. You know how automatic systems can have errors when you travel a series of routes with specific conditions? To put it simply, it's a security hole—tell it to turn right and turn left at the same time, give it any contradictory conditions, and its decision-making functions will dull. The HsPS-15 just got displayed in an interceptor weaponry exhibit. Did you forget it was a prototype?"

To make matters worse, this version of the powered suit was built to share everything. In other words, if one malfunctioned, they'd all be affected.

Tsuchimikado drew close to one stopped powered suit, then wrenched the anti-bulkhead shotgun out of the machine's arms. "…One drive compensator's error will propagate to all the rest. If you want to get out, you'll have to switch the ejection function to manual and do it yourself. It's an annoying process, too, so it'll take you ten minutes at the least," he said, putting the huge shotgun, which looked like a sawed-off tank cannon, on his shoulders.

The people inside the powered suits seemed to be listening to him in shock. Not even they knew about their machines' issues, so how did this man? They couldn't imagine the answer.

Meanwhile, Tsuchimikado gave a punch to a nearby powered suit's armor and continued, fed up with them. "If you're going to come out, hurry up. If the Avignon rioters know you won't attack them, they'll be all over you in a heartbeat."

With those words, he began to hear creaks and clangs from inside the suits. They seemed to be considerably panicked. Tsuchimikado thought to himself as he watched them.

Now then… He'd succeeded at temporarily disabling the powered suits, but the soldiers themselves weren't dead. *This is where the real deal starts*, he thought.

For now, they were immobile until they restored their ejection functions and came out. Once they were out of their combat states, he could talk with them, too.

Should I explain that I'm an Academy City spy first? No, wait, I'm acting out of line with the higher-ups' intentions. Jeez, I hope I can discuss this without making things worse.

As Tsuchimikado mulled over how his negotiating should go, his thoughts came to a halt and he abruptly looked up.

A roar.

His eyes showed him jet-black bombers circling leisurely through the blue skies.

There was more than one of the one-hundred-meter-class aircraft. Over ten bombers were drawing wide flight arcs around Avignon airspace.

The sight of their unique silhouettes made Tsuchimikado clench his teeth. *Academy City's HsB-02…Our supersonic stealth bombers?!*

He and Kamijou had used a supersonic passenger plane that could produce speeds of over seven thousand kilometers per hour to get to Avignon. These stealth bombers used the same technology. With their incomparable speed, it was said they could shake off homing missiles just by flying straight.

Thinking calmly, there had been just one issue: the question of where on earth all these powered suits in Avignon had come from.

This was the answer.

Bombers from Academy City loaded with powered suits had carried them to France in an hour, and they'd dropped them all with parachutes into Avignon's outskirts. It was an incredible feat of brute force, but Academy City's elaborate technologies had made it possible.

Of course, the HsB-02s were loaded up with more than that. They would have what they needed to do what they were meant to do: bombing runs.

Damn..., he cursed, glaring up into the sky. *They dropped the powered suits first to make sure the Document of Constantine was here in Avignon. Now that they have, are they going to use those bombers to blow the entire Papal Palace away?!* .

It was a crude, easy-to-understand mission, but given the effects of the unique spell Terra of the Left possessed, it was hard to imagine the mission bearing any certain results.

With a *bang*, Tsuchimikado slammed on one of the powered suits' armor. "Hey! How is the evacuation of Avignon's citizens going?! When are they carrying out the bombing?! Don't tell me they're using the brand-new HsB-02s so they can use *that* here!!"

As he shouted, he felt impatience creeping into his mind. *What are you thinking, Aleister? The others aside, you know full well what the sorcery world is like. If you could completely settle everything with normal military action, there would be no groups like Necessarius around. Did you not realize this wouldn't be enough to be sure you'd destroy the Document of Constantine?*

Or, he thought, a different idea coming to him, *could you...have yet another trick up your sleeve?*

5

Nine thousand meters above Avignon.

Inside one of the eleven HsB-02 supersonic stealth bombers rode a Level Five esper with a cane. Normally, the large space would have been loaded with bombs, but here, only the Level Five and several maintenance crew members were present.

A shrill alarm bell and messages full of static came over the speakers attached to the bomber's interior. Hearing this, one of the maintenance crew members turned to look at the Level Five.

"Operational objective A accomplished! Now moving to operation B. When operation C begins, this partition will open. Get your parachute ready!!"

"Don't need it," answered the Level Five tiredly to the maintenance crew member.

The Level Five was relaxed as he leaned on his cane, staring at the thin monitor attached to the wall of the craft.

Man, this is such a pain. I'm a busy man, you know. Who told them they could start shooting things up outside Academy City? God, just let me get this crap out of the way and get back to the real stuff.

Avignon seen from the skies above was a small town surrounded by old walls. The tall buildings inside it looked crammed into a confused jumble, probably because the walls limited the amount of land available.

The Level Five saw it and chuckled. "Ha-ha. Just like a miniature Academy City."

"What?"

"Nothing. When did the world get this convenient? Seriously, one hour to fly from Academy City to France?"

"I-it's not all convenient," responded the crew member to the Level Five, choosing his words carefully. "For supersonic aircraft, the drag causes the exterior surface temperature to skyrocket. At top speed, it can get close to one thousand degrees, so liquid coolant pipes have to be strung up all throughout the craft."

"Liquid oxygen and liquid hydrogen?"

"Yes. Pipes with low-freezing-point coolant go through these tanks to amplify the coolant's effects. This liquid oxygen and hydrogen is also used for space shuttle propellant, and this craft uses it as one of its fuel sources…In other words, the more fuel runs out, the more coolant effects it loses."

"Which is why you were saying we were stopping at London on the way back instead of just making a U-turn. Can't believe you got permission to let this bomber get refueled. Japan isn't even allowed to have bombers in the first place," he said, astonished, as another alarm bell came over the in-flight speakers.

After hearing the announcement, the maintenance crew member raised his voice. "Beginning operation B!!"

As he spoke, four of the bombers flying nearby veered from their circling course.

They flew some fifteen kilometers away in a turn, slowly expanding their circle's radius. Then their noses turned, and they abruptly accelerated.

The four aircraft were tracking through the air together in a square formation, and there was a piece attached to those bombers that was different from the one the Level Five rode in:

Jet-black blades, half the total length of the aircraft.

The blades could retract and extend like police batons. Their surfaces, made to compress electricity, featured patterns and irregularities that could be controlled on the micrometer level.

The massively long and delicate blades began to swing around from the supersonic bomber's acceleration force, slicing through the skies at over seven thousand kilometers per hour.

Just that made the generated downward-facing blades insanely destructive.

If a small amount of iron sand was also mixed into those atmospheric blades, what would happen?

The answer appeared a moment later.

Crsshwoosh!!

The four bombers carved a square into the land around the town of Avignon.

The blades' surfaces had only scattered a few grams of iron sand.

But with their immense speed of over ten thousand kilometers per hour, the metal powder had skipped melting and vaporized. Despite being kilometers up in the air, the gaseous blades cleaved into the earth with a temperature exceeding eight thousand degrees Celsius, leaving an orange glow behind.

Guh-chunk!! The bomber the Level Five rode on shook.

A friendly supersonic bomber had passed by them, stirring up turbulence.

"...!"

The Level Five placed a hand on the nearby wall but didn't take his eyes off the monitor.

The first thing to be created was a ditch, twenty meters wide and over ten deep. Immediately after, those ditches melted in the orange and collapsed. The geology itself was roiling like magma. In a flash, the ancient city of Avignon was isolated by a river of molten rock. It cut off electrical lines and water pipes, and even forced apart the flow of the river Rhone passing near the town. Flooding was already starting to occur around the town's outskirts.

With this, the people in the ancient city of Avignon were completely trapped.

The town extended beyond Avignon's ramparts, too. He remembered hearing that the powered suits had forcibly removed civilians from the areas that were now molten lava beforehand, but he was pretty sure nobody was about to thank them.

Hah. Just three kilograms of iron sand, and those Earthslicers can rip apart all of Eurasia in an hour. Academy City's making some interesting stuff.

Normally, bombers had an escort of several fighter craft. Unlike the smaller jets, hulking bombers couldn't make tight turns. If one tried, it would immediately decelerate, and if things were really bad, its momentum could crush the plane and it would break apart in midair. If an enemy got a lock on one, it had no way to dodge the missiles. It could fool the lock to a certain extent with things like chaffs and flares, but those weren't perfect, either. Therefore, the only option was to station fighters around the bombers as an escort to help them avoid missile locks.

Those rules, however, didn't apply to these supersonic HsB-02 bombers.

If all they could do was go straight, they'd make a plane that could shake off missiles just by flying ahead.

They would make it happen by giving it the overwhelming speed of seven thousand kilometers per hour. Air-to-air missiles fired by fighters were nothing, and even ground-to-air missiles waiting beforehand at the bombing point would barely have time to acquire a lock before the bombing run was done and the bombers were already outside missile range.

High-speed bombing tactics that defeated the old rules of air combat with brute force. Add Academy City's own high-efficiency stealth tech to the mix, and it became virtually impossible to stop an HsB-02's attack before it happened.

"Isolation of operational area confirmed!!" shouted one of the aircraft crew.

The bombers that fired the Earthslicers got a good twenty kilometers out and began to decelerate. Meanwhile, they stopped creating any downward wind currents, probably because they adjusted the patterns on the surface of their blades.

"Now beginning aerial bombing of all operational areas, including the objective zone!!"

The Earthslicers appeared to be an extremely unsubtle attack, but by electrically manipulating the "pattern" on the blade's surface, the bomber could make attacks not only in a straight line, but in arcs and pinpoints as well, able to deliver surgical destruction like cutting pieces out of a jigsaw puzzle. If they wanted to, a single bomber seemed to be able to create several lines simultaneously, too.

"This bomber's course will now change to secure a flight route for the eight units conducting the bombing. Brace for sudden impact!"

Their next attack target was the old city of Avignon itself.

The target wasn't just a single building like the Papal Palace, but the entire region they called the "ancient city." The powered suits that had dropped earlier were there as well, but the pilots had a sort of transmitter. That signal alone was enough for the bombers to avoid those spots while burning the rest of Avignon to the ground. The pilots would pretend to be locals and move to the nearby Mediterranean shoreline, then use submarines stationed there to leave France. It would obviously be too conspicuous to go long distances while wearing the powered suits, so they'd have to leave the irretrievable equipment on-site and destroy them.

But if the operation went as planned, the grounded forces would have to get through the sea of molten rock on their own. They probably had some kind of gear for that, too. The entire city would conveniently be turned to lava around them, and it would create something of an updraft, so maybe they planned to use portable gear that applied the principle of dandelion fluff and go for a little sight-seeing flight.

"..." As far as he could tell from the monitor, there were still quite a few people in the ancient city of Avignon who were late to escape. Those lucky enough to be near the forces would be saved, but most of them would be burned down by the eight-thousand-degree blades.

"Change of plans."

"What?"

"We're after the Papal Palace, right? Focus your attack on that first. If you still don't get results, I'll go down. And if you lose contact with me, then you can go ahead and bomb the entire ancient city."

"I, well...The Level Five drop operation is categorized under operation C. Normally defeating the enemy forces is calculated under operation B, so—"

"Change of plans," repeated the Level Five.

The crewman's spine stiffened. He must have just remembered why this Level Five was on the bomber.

He was their bomb.

And like a nuclear bomb or a hydrogen bomb, he was loaded on the big bomber to be dropped into the mission's operation area.

The crew member grabbed the radio in his lap and started communicating with someone. He seemed to be negotiating with the higher-ups handling the operation, and after repeating the exchange several times, he put the radio down and quietly looked at the Level Five.

"...R-request accepted. We're changing our plans for operation B and focusing our attacks on the Papal Palace."

His face was clearly baffled as to why his stubborn superiors had accepted so easily. Meanwhile, the corners of the Level Five's lips turned up. "That's fine."

"B-but how will you…?" asked the man.

The Level Five tsked, unamused. The monitor showed the isolated town of Avignon and the people fleeing like little grains of rice. "Maybe it's all the same to you, but there's different types and levels of evil."

An electronic tone echoed through the craft—they were probably starting the procedure to open the partition. As he listened to it, the Level Five spoke to the crew member.

"And first-rate villains don't go after honest people."

6

A roaring sound, many times louder than sprinkling cold water on a burning-hot metal plate, reverberated through the Papal Palace.

Something seemed to be happening outside the building, but neither Kamijou nor Itsuwa nor Terra looked outside.

Kamijou got his right fist ready and glared at Terra.

About seven meters separated them; he was already inside the range of Terra's flour guillotine. Plus, he had his special prioritization effects.

The floor was in poor shape. Fragments of the stone wall Terra had shattered were scattered about, along with several cylindrical shells that must have been from the defeated powered suit.

"I'll ask one last time. Any intent on handing over the document quietly?"

"No, none at all. Please die the warrior's death you desire."

Upon hearing that, Kamijou sprinted forward.

Terra matched his movement by swinging the flour blade in his right hand.

Kamijou stuck out his right hand, taking up a defensive posture while running, but…

"Prioritize—atmosphere as lower, flour as higher."

Shoom!! With a roar, the weapon instantly expanded.

Now a giant fan shape about three meters across, the guillotine flew toward Kamijou, engulfing a ton of air on the way.

"?!"

Kamijou couldn't react.

Itsuwa, who had run for Terra at the same time as him, grabbed onto Kamijou's arm. She jumped, dragging him to the side, and a moment later, the "mere air" that shouldn't have had any hardness or sharpness to it ripped through the floor and wall of the Papal Palace. Several shells littered about the floor burst like fireworks. The blast was like a shock wave and almost made him choke.

Itsuwa gently let go of his arm.

Then, with motions unimaginably quick considering that act, she put up the spear in her hands again and drove it at Terra's throat like an iron stake.

Boom!! The sound of air splitting apart rang out.

"Prioritize—blade as lower, human skin as higher."

With a few words from Terra, Itsuwa's attack bounced off his skin.

Only the *geen!!* sound of vibrating metal echoed through the Papal Palace.

A stinging pain engulfed Itsuwa's hands, as though she'd stabbed a boulder.

But she didn't stop moving.

Her spear still flat, she kicked up a small rock at her feet, launching it sharply at Terra's eyes.

Terra didn't turn his head; he didn't even close his eyes.

Instead, he casually swung his arm.

The horizontal sweep plunged toward the rock, Itsuwa, and Kamijou—who was charging in from another angle—as well, forcing them all back a distance.

With a dull *wham!!* Kamijou and Itsuwa were thrown to the floor.

As she tried to get back up, the girl grimaced. "Ow…?!"

They had fallen into a spot with a great amount of debris from the wall Terra had destroyed. She'd fallen on top of it, and it had damaged her ankle.

And Terra wasn't about to let that go by. "Prioritize—human flesh as lower, flour as higher."

The guillotine flew.

Itsuwa, who couldn't move with her hurt foot, immediately brought her spear up.

Just then, Kamijou broke in from the side.

He stuck out his right hand, sending Terra's attack scattering in all directions.

A thunderous *roar!!* sounded.

When Terra tried to swing his right arm again, this time Itsuwa shoved Kamijou to the side, then pushed off her injured foot to jump in the other direction.

Terra's guillotine crashed into the spot between them.

"Oh, how valiant," said Terra with a short laugh, staring at Itsuwa as she held in her pain. "But you're at your limit. Dragging your heels…in a literal sense."

Those words made Kamijou flare up.

Itsuwa, though, stated, "…Yes." Yet there was a smile on her lips. "But you finally showed an opening. A critical one."

"Whatever do you mean?"

"That thing Mr. Tsuchimikado was about to say. The priority spell you're so good at, Light's Execution—it has a weakness. He was right. There was something unnatural about what you did just now…"

"Oh?" said Terra offhandedly, amused.

Itsuwa slowly leveled her spearhead at Terra. "The Amakusa-Style Crossist Church doesn't use any incantations or magic circles. Instead, we combine magical symbols left over in everyday items and customs. Looking for those symbols is what we're good at."

"I see. That is indeed troubling," said Terra emotionlessly. "Still, there's no time for you to apply that knowledge now that you've real- ized it, I think?"

Terra raised his right hand above his head.

The guillotine there sharpened like a screw and drove up toward the high ceiling.

"Prioritize—ceiling as lower, flour as higher."

And when his hand jerked, as if to pull a light cord, it came.

Tug.

Like a trap in an old castle, the ceiling on this floor suddenly came tumbling down.

The pillars supporting the ceiling began to sink into the floor with unnatural smoothness.

"!!" Itsuwa hastily put her spear straight up.

It stuck between the fallen ceiling and the floor, allowing them to just barely avoid being crushed to death.

But because of that, Itsuwa no longer had her weapon.

And that was when…

Terra's guillotine came swooping mercilessly in.

A booming roar burst out.

Terra's blade came in horizontally and landed directly on Itsuwa's unarmed torso. She bent over at the impact, and with a dull sound, her body went flying back. It bounced a few times on the floor, rolled several meters away, and finally lost its momentum, coming to a stop.

She stayed down, body limp.

Her arms and legs were sprawled out. Kamijou could see her chest slowly rising and falling, so she didn't appear to be dead yet, but it didn't look like she'd wake up anytime soon.

Damn it…, thought Kamijou, gritting his back teeth. "Itsuwa!!"

"Well, that's about how it is. A simple sorcerer thinking she could stand up to God's Right Seat was a mistake to begin with," boasted Terra as the fallen ceiling slowly began to rise back to its former height. The compressed pillars started returning to their original lengths as well.

Itsuwa's spear, which had avoided being crushed, clattered to the floor.

"You…" Kamijou slowly, slowly began to tighten his right fist.

But even upon seeing his face, Terra didn't look any less calm. "Oh my. It won't do me any good if you get angry like that. We're in the middle of a battle. I'm sure you're not about to tell me to hold still and not attack so you can keep punching me forever, yes?"

"..."

"And I must say, I'm quite disappointed myself. With a name like Imagine Breaker, I thought I'd have a more difficult time of it, but I hadn't thought it was so imperfect. If its original abilities were restored, you could have easily protected that sorcerer from my attack."

"What?" Kamijou frowned.

The Imagine Breaker—its original abilities.

Kamijou unwittingly looked at his right hand. Terra saw it and gave a thin smile.

"Oh. Could it be that you don't know?"

"!"

"Keh-heh...Well now, that can't be possible. Normally, you would *need* to know about it. Which means...hmm? Could it be...*that you don't remember something that you should have known?*"

"You!!"

"Was I spot on? Oh my. I seem to have found myself an entertaining research subject indeed!!"

"...!!"

Maybe it was illogical to get angry right now.

But for Kamijou, who was an amnesiac, those words were enough to bore a hole into his heart.

"Ha-ha!!" Terra burst out laughing as he watched his adversary manage to wobble up to his feet. "I see, I see, so that's how it is! I certainly don't recall any reports to that effect, but...Could you have been hiding it? What for? Did you make sure to tell that sorcerer taking a rest over there? Maybe it would be interesting to look into why you lost your memories, hmm?"

Damn it all!!

Anger dominated Kamijou.

He had decided not to tell anybody he'd lost his memories for the sake of the girl in white—the first person he'd met after losing them. That was the rule he gave himself. It was something he had to uphold. That rule being broken now, and like this, was enough to almost drive him mad.

"Well, what's the problem?" Terra of the Left laughed. "You're about to die anyway, so why bother worrying? I don't know what's getting you so gloomy, but I'll do you a favor and get rid of it all."

With slow motions, Terra brought his blade up. Kamijou clenched his back teeth so hard he thought he'd break them.

...That blade's destructive power isn't the fatal part, he thought, glaring at the white powder roiling around Terra. *The problem is that prioritizing thing...He can use it for both attack and defense. If I can find a weakness in it—if there really is one—I can use it to drive him back!!*

Both Tsuchimikado and Itsuwa had declared that there *was* one.

It could have also been a riposte to Terra of the Left—or more simply, a mere bluff.

No, there's something, he thought, gauging the distance between them. *Now that I think about it, Terra's attacks* have *been somehow strange. But I was brushing it off as a fortunate miscalculation and didn't really think about it. How he...*

"Oh, you won't be coming to me?" mocked Terra, waggling his flour guillotine. "Then waiting for you would be a pain. Allow me to make the first move!!"

He flung the white blade as he finished speaking.

And as Touma Kamijou watched it come right before his eyes, he...

7

Shwoom!! As the flour blade came rushing at him, Kamijou didn't bring his right hand to meet it.

Instead, he swung his head out of the way to dodge the strike.

As he did, he bent backward as though falling to the floor and picked up a fragment of the ruined wall—a rock the size of a bento box.

Then he rose again, flinging it at Terra like a counterattack.

"Prioritize—building stone as lower, human skin as higher," sung Terra.

The rock hit him in the forehead, but he didn't even blink.

At the same time, Kamijou's hand dove into his pants pocket. Terra's eyes sharpened. Kamijou ignored it, grabbing what was in there and hurling it straight at him.

The flour guillotine howled.

But when he looked at what its tip had just sliced, he frowned.

It was a simple wallet.

Kamijou had thrown a piece of leather with no use as a weapon at all. When he saw Terra's reaction, he spoke. "I wonder why that is." His words were cutting. "You could have easily turned away Itsuwa's spear and Tsuchimikado's spell, so why didn't you block a simple wallet with your prioritization?"

"...?!" Terra flung his flour guillotine at him, as though trying to shut him up.

Kamijou turned it aside with his right hand and went on. "Now that I think of it, it was strange."

He stepped forward, cutting through the powdery remains of the guillotine.

"It was strange how Itsuwa and I are both still alive after getting hit with that white blade. You've got no reason to hold back, and you don't seem the type to let the loser get away. Which makes things simple. When you slashed us with the blade, it wasn't that you purposely left us alive. *It was that you couldn't actually kill us, no matter what you did.*"

The force of that swinging blade alone wasn't enough to kill a person because Terra was using his prioritization spell to strengthen it.

Which meant...

"Your prioritization isn't very flexible. Your blade always lost strength right after you stopped one of our attacks. Which means *you can't use it against multiple targets at once.* If you want to change from one prioritization to another, you have to set it up every single time. Something like that, right?"

"Heh," chuckled Terra. The corners of his lips softened, and he brought his giant blade up again. "So that was what you lot meant by the Light's Execution's 'weakness.'"

He almost sounded relieved that the mystery had been solved.

"After all, I haven't fully adjusted it yet. I will admit I was somewhat interested in what you had to say."

The clergyman smiled.

"However," he went on, flipping back into his typical scorn, "so what if you've figured it out? Terra of the Left isn't so weak that you could defeat him like that!!"

With the sound of ripping wind, the white blade flew.

Kamijou blocked it with his hand, and as Terra backstepped to gain distance, he chased.

"Terra!!" he shouted, but the man was faster. He swung the flour guillotine again, bringing it stabbing straight down.

"Prioritize—floor as lower, flour as higher."

The thick stone floor was blown away, and its fragments rushed at Kamijou. He jumped aside to dodge them. "What's the reason you're going this far?! You got not only us but everyone in Avignon wrapped up in this! Is whatever you're doing really worth all this?!"

"Hah, I do believe half the blame belongs with your Academy City, am I wrong?!" answered Terra, retreating with short hops and gathering the floury powder at his hands. "All of Crossism shares one final goal—the kingdom of heaven."

"What?"

"Oh, but were you of a Crossist culture, you'd know it better than the colors on traffic lights. Well, you do seem to be from a Far Eastern island nation, where organized religion runs thin, so I suppose there's no helping it."

Terra spoke with light boredom and disappointment.

"After the Last Judgment, God will build a new kingdom with his own hands. Only those whose faith runs deep will be permitted a sojourn in its eternal salvation. Don't you think it's truly wonderful? That is where I aim, and I was fortunate enough to help others toward that same goal."

Terra fired the flour guillotine, and Kamijou repelled it with his right hand.

Several of the cylindrical shells on the floor began rolling around with the wind pressure.

As he watched his weapon scatter into powder, he said, "But then I had a thought, you see."

No wind was blowing, but the powder began to return to Terra's hand unnaturally and systematically.

"Wouldn't man wage war in this holy land? Even if God built a perfect kingdom and called together the faithful and just from around the world, would the group called mankind be able to answer God's expectations?"

Kamijou ran forward, listening.

Terra flung his guillotine to stop him. "Suppose I lead the faithful of Crossism to this holy land. But even the Roman Orthodox Church is separated into countless factions. If God used the search condition of 'only pious Roman Orthodox followers' to grant salvation, it would mean the Church's faction problems would carry over into that land."

The flour wriggled in concert with Terra's right hand and changed into a giant blade.

The white guillotine and Kamijou's fist collided.

"...No matter how perfect the kingdom God builds, if the humans inside it break up in an unsightly way, what's the point? If we brought the same old wars into this so-called perfect kingdom, everything will have been for nothing. You cannot call that 'eternal salvation.'"

Even as Kamijou nullified the flour guillotine with his right hand, he listened.

Terra, too, moved forward, realizing it was pointless to retreat any farther.

"We want salvation. And I want to give salvation. Even if God's plan is perfect, if we, mankind, fall below his expectations, everything will start over! I want to know!! Is humanity doomed to warring within the holy land as we stand now? And if so, I want to know what direction I should steer everyone in before the Day of Judgment!

"And that is why I am in God's Right Seat!!" he roared.

Unlike his fellow member Vento of the Front, he had chosen this path himself, for the sake of the Roman Orthodox Church. If he had gone that far, then maybe he really was trying to protect all those who believed in the institution.

But...

"...Is that all salvation is?" asked Kamijou, unwittingly clenching his back teeth.

The face of Monaka Oyafune came to mind, who had taken a bullet to get him to act.

He thought about Tsuchimikado and Itsuwa, who had fought alongside him.

"It's not like the Church is wrong. I don't think the teachings of the Church that raised Orsola and Agnes have grown into this. You've got a problem before that. You have no idea what the word *salvation* even means!"

The rioters all about the town of Avignon.

The powered suits that had come to suppress them and been crushed by this man.

"There's no way your God spread teachings so that they would create this kind of war! That's bullshit. If you insist on redefining what salvation means so that it satisfies you alone..."

He simply set his eyes forward, sending a glare at the man before him.

There was his enemy.

"...then I'll tear down that screwed-up illusion here and now!!"

Kamijou dove at Terra.

The man retreated farther, readying his guillotine. At this rate, Kamijou would never catch up, no matter how long he chased.

But he advanced anyway.

The bottom of his foot caught a powered suit shell on the floor, but he ignored it and stepped forward with even more force.

Then he used all his might to kick something at his feet ahead.

It was the Friulian spear Itsuwa had dropped.

The spear didn't get kicked up easily and went sliding across the floor. It collided with the barrel of an anti-bulkhead shotgun that a powered suit dropped; its trajectory curved somewhat but still slipped toward Terra's feet.

"!!" Terra swung down his guillotine and smashed Itsuwa's spear. He could have avoided the attack simply by lifting his foot, but he expressly used the guillotine to block it.

Just like I thought. Meanwhile, Kamijou stepped even closer to Terra, sharply making his way toward the man, more deeply than he'd been able to get thus far. *If Terra himself had so much strength to begin with, he wouldn't need that whole "priority switching" magic at all. He wouldn't have to switch them; people at the top were already at their highest point. It doesn't mean they have high physical abilities. In other words...*

Kamijou's conclusion was reached.

He poured every ounce of strength into his right fist.

...Terra of the Left isn't strong at all. This bastard's just been watching from a safe distance, pretending he's strong. But there's no way he's stronger than Itsuwa or me, when we've actually been on the battlefield personally!

After smashing Itsuwa's spear to the floor, Terra countered, muttering his "priorities" and launching his flour guillotine. But Kamijou's right fist destroyed the attack.

"You're too slow!!"

His fist flew at Terra's face.

A dull *wham!!* burst out.

He felt his tightly clenched fist make a direct hit from the recoil.

He'd put all his weight into his right arm, so his body pitched forward.

I got you!! he thought, confident.

But Terra didn't go down.

"You…bastard…You heretic monkeeeeeeeeeeeeeey!!"

With an angry scream, the man's strength returned.

The scraping sound of shoe soles resounded on the floor. Terra's foot got caught on a powered suit, almost tripping. He lost his balance and leaned back, but his will to fight hadn't broken. He swung his right hand from his unstable position, sending the flour guillotine stabbing toward Kamijou's gut with all his might.

"Prioritize—human body as lower, flour as higher!!"

The blade he fired had been set to cleave a human.

Meanwhile, Kamijou punched Terra in the face again, sending him flying.

In this state, it would be hard to repel the guillotine with his right hand. The same went for twisting himself out of the way.

—!! Kamijou suddenly stomped hard on an object at his feet.

It was an extremely thick-barreled anti-bulkhead shotgun—the one from the powered suit Terra had destroyed.

The shotgun was on an oblique angle atop a pile of debris, and when Kamijou stomped on it, it swerved like a seesaw, the hunk of metal standing straight up in front of him in reaction.

"That is…quite naïve of you!!"

But Terra's expression didn't change.

The anti-bulkhead shotgun was heavy and not easily brought to bear. Even if Kamijou had grabbed onto the giant firearm, it would take seconds before his hands could aim it in this state and pull the trigger on his enemy.

His desperate recovery had failed. Terra's guillotine crashed toward Kamijou's side, encompassing the anti-bulkhead shotgun he'd frantically tried to grab as it went.

A tremendous *sha-bam!!* echoed throughout the Papal Palace.

Red blood flew.

The slimy liquid dropped from Kamijou's mouth as he doubled over. Unable to block it with his right hand, unable to twist himself

out of the way, he had taken the hit straight to the gut. Energy seeped from his body.

"Wha...?"

A gasp.

But Kamijou wasn't the one who produced it; it came from Terra of the Left's mouth.

It was only natural. He'd strengthened his guillotine with his prioritization spell, and yet *Kamijou's body hadn't come apart in two pieces.*

"..." Kamijou grinned and tightened his right fist around the guillotine poking into his stomach.

That was all it took to blow the flour blade to smithereens.

Terra tried to retreat, but Kamijou stepped forward before that.

He was within firing range of his fist now.

"This result is absolute nonsense...The Imagine Breaker should only work in your right hand. What happened? Could this heretic monk have possibly already...that power—?!"

"It's nothing like that," said Kamijou, clenching his right fist tightly. "This didn't have anything to do with that."

"Then—?!" Terra tried to shout, but Kamijou moved first.

He aimed straight at Terra of the Left's face, colored by shock as it was.

"Think I'll answer you?"

A dull *whump!!* rang out.

This time, Terra's body hit the floor.

8

"Urgh..." Kamijou held his stinging belly, strengthened his wobbling legs, and managed to prop himself upright. The guillotine hadn't torn his abdomen, but there was a nice bruise there expanding to quite a range.

I'm saved...somehow.

As he looked at the anti-bulkhead shotgun, twisted from the impact, and Itsuwa's spear nearby, he breathed a sigh of relief. The last flour guillotine Terra had thrown out…The attack aimed at him should have, of course, been loaded with the spell saying "prioritize the guillotine's strength over Kamijou's body." If it had landed directly, it probably would have easily torn through his gut.

But Kamijou was alive—thanks to the powered suit's anti-bulkhead shotgun, which he'd kicked upright at the last second.

Terra's prioritization was strong, certainly, but the priority could only apply to one type of item. To change the priority from one item to another, he had to reset the conditions every time.

In other words, in a state where the guillotine's strength was prioritized over Kamijou's body, it wouldn't particularly affect anything *besides* his body. If you stuck a different object between Kamijou's body and the guillotine, the guillotine would stop. Things like air or wallets were soft to begin with, so they wouldn't do much, but the shotgun was made of metal.

The guillotine's natural power wouldn't let it rupture internal organs, even with a direct hit. Using something with decent hardness as a shield made it easy to block the attack.

The bottleneck was that he didn't know how far the spell would apply the prioritization to his body…but leaving his clothing and his possessions aside, it didn't seem to treat other people's possessions—the powered suit's anti-bulkhead shotgun—as part of his body.

Even Itsuwa's spear, which he'd kicked at Terra right before that, was someone else's possession, like the shotgun. That was why Terra couldn't cleave both the spear and Kamijou's body in two at once. If Kamijou normally carried around a spear, though, it would have been treated as his.

That spear had been how Kamijou realized Terra's weakness. Without it, Kamijou's body would be in two pieces right now.

"…" He gazed down at Terra, lying on the floor.

All that flour, unable to maintain its shape as a blade, was scattered around him.

One way or another, it's over...Is Itsuwa okay? And Tsuchimikado...
*He could still be fighting the powered suits...*Kamijou looked at the white grains slowly blowing away on the wind, having lost their magical efficacy.

As he endured the pain, he still breathed a sigh of relief.

He looked at Terra again.

A cylindrical item had rolled out of Terra's clothing and onto the floor. It was a rolled-up piece of old parchment, the Document of Constantine—a powerful Soul Arm.

Kamijou stooped down and grabbed it up with his right hand.

Actually, it crumbled before he grasped it.

As soon as Kamijou's fingertips touched the document, the parchment tore apart like ashes tapped away from a cigarette. As it crumbled into powder, a gentle breeze swept it away to who knew where.

It was all so very quick.

Enough to make the ruckus up until now feel empty.

Kamijou diverted his attention from the lost Document of Constantine and began to think about the enemy he'd been fighting until now.

...Terra, huh?

He looked down at the unconscious man lying there.

This wasn't Academy City. He couldn't leave their fight's cleanup to Anti-Skill. He couldn't let his guard down until he was certain he'd restrained Terra and taken him to where he needed to go.

Come to think of it, I wonder if Tsuchimikado's doing all right. I should contact him and talk it over with the Puritans for now. Partly because I get the feeling Academy City doesn't have much influence here...

The powered suits that had assaulted Avignon were Academy City–made, but strangely, Kamijou didn't consider discussing this with them. Maybe their first impression had been too terrible for him.

He looked around.

Itsuwa was lying a short distance away.

He approached, then grabbed her delicate shoulders and gently shook her, but she showed no signs of waking. Regular breathing was coming from her lips, though, and her chest was rising and falling slightly.

"Oh, right. Her spear…"

Kamijou went to pick up the spear he'd kicked away, then returned to Itsuwa's side.

He gently placed the dangerous-looking blade right next to her.

"Thanks, Itsuwa. If you hadn't been here, I don't think I could have won," he said quietly to the girl with her eyes shut.

Terra had taken her out, so she hadn't heard those things he and Kamijou had talked about regarding his amnesia…probably. But he wasn't happy about it. She'd helped him and fought beside him without knowing any of that, after all.

"…"

Only bitter things were in his heart.

But for now, Kamijou shook it off. *Anyway, let's talk to Tsuchimikado…*

He thought about calling him on his cell phone, but despite looking in his pocket, it wasn't there. He looked around and saw what seemed to be it lying on the floor a few steps away.

But when he picked it up, the LCD was too far gone to see anything, and he couldn't close it, either; some part was probably blocking it.

"Damn," he muttered, before hearing a rustling behind him.

"!!"

He wheeled on his heel, but Terra was still lying on the floor. However, his arm was in a slightly different position. He must have tried to get up but didn't have the strength.

"Ha-ha. I see. Yes, the Imagine Breaker has terrible compatibility with us. It cancels out everything, as though rejecting all the hard work we've put in," he said, lips moving slowly as he lay on the floor and glared resentfully at Kamijou. "…Will you not ask?"

"Ask what?"

"About the Imagine Breaker."

The words took him by surprise, and Kamijou paused for a moment. The Imagine Breaker.

He'd been using it like it was nothing this whole time, never having any real doubts about the power. But Terra had said he knew something about it; did that mean it wasn't of the science side but of the sorcery side? But Index, who had 103,000 grimoires memorized, didn't appear to know what it really was.

He thought for a moment. "Do you know?"

"Keh-heh," sneered Terra of the Left cruelly. "Asking me for confirmation…It would seem you really have lost your memory."

"…"

"Heh-heh. You should give some thought as to why the Imagine Breaker is within your right hand. Therein lies an important answer. Still, its effect of nullifying any sorcery without question has meaning as well…"

Terra watched Kamijou wonder, then smiled, amused.

Then he spoke:

"It's a simple matter."

The slight sigh Terra gave rang awfully loud in Kamijou's ears.

Slowly, the man's lips moved.

"The Imagine Breaker is actually—"

Kamijou couldn't make out the next words.

Because with a massive *boom!!*…

…Terra's body suddenly exploded.

Actually, strictly speaking, Kamijou hadn't seen the moment itself.

An orange flash of light had plunged through the ceiling and fallen right on top of the man. As soon as the three-meter-wide pillar of light pierced the floor, an incredible wind blasted through the room in the Papal Palace.

Kamijou's feet were instantly peeled from the floor, and he was blown several meters backward like a ball of dust. Itsuwa and the powered suit, lying in other places, took the blast in the same fashion and rolled toward him.

"Gwaaaaaaaaaaaaaaaaahhhhhhhhhhhhh?!"

Kamijou screamed as he was slammed into the floor.

Apart from that overall injury, he felt a thin, stinging pain shoot up his arm. It felt like the day after getting sunburned. He looked and saw that the skin had reddened. It was burned.

Wh-what...?

He shook his hazy head and looked over to where the blast had hit. Then his body went rigid.

The place Terra had been lying just a moment ago had already changed to a vortex of molten rock. Over several meters, the floor made of stone had changed into a muddy swamp shining orange, and from the ceiling with a big hole in it as well, the same kind of thing was dripping. He heard the sizzling sound of water evaporating. Simply trying to get near, a hot blast like an invisible wall clung to his skin.

He looked around and spotted something out the window.

Circling slowly, as though creating black smudges against the blue sky—multiple bombers.

Instead of their bulkheads for dropping bombs, they had jet-black metal blades. He didn't know what had happened, but it was clear they'd carried out some sort of attack.

"Terra..."

Still unable to get very close to the wall of heat, Kamijou called the name of the man who had been his enemy.

The steel wings dancing in the skies once again set their sights on this place.

The bombers, which had used a sufficient approach distance to accelerate, darted through the air at incredible speeds.

"Terraaaaaaaaaaaaaaaaaaaaaaaaaaaaaaaaaaaaaaaaa!!"

His scream was drowned out.

Several pillars of light flashed down through the ceiling, again pinpointing the exact spot Terra had been.

Their precision might have been closer to sniping than bombing. The orange light blocked out his vision. Taking some kind of aftershock, Kamijou's body bounded over the floor again and again.

That was when he passed out.

But even if he hadn't, he wouldn't have found Terra again.

From the section in front of the fallen Kamijou, the walls and ceiling had disappeared, all replaced by a sea of lava. A third of the Papal Palace had been lost.

...And Terra of the Left had vanished, leaving not even a corpse behind.

EPILOGUE

That Answer Leads to the Next Mystery
Question.

The impact woke Itsuwa up.

She was in the Papal Palace. Right before she'd lost consciousness, she'd fallen into the middle of the floor...or so she'd thought, but when she awoke, she had rolled near a wall. The spear she'd been using was close by, as well.

Her whole body felt sluggish and hard to move, probably because the damage remained.

With slow movements, she took her spear.

Itsuwa thought to herself that her body felt flushed. A moment later, she realized why.

In front of her.

The stone walls, floor, and ceiling some ten meters ahead were melted by high heat, having changed into an orange plasma. She heard a sizzling sound, like from water dripping onto an iron; most of her view was blocked by whitish steam.

"What...what happened...?"

She observed her surroundings.

A short distance away lay the unmoving powered suit. Near it, the Imagine Breaker boy was lying faceup. He didn't seem to be conscious. She approached and saw redness on his skin. He was more than flushed—he seemed to have light burns.

This degree probably wouldn't leave scars, but it would be nice if she had some ice. Of course, she didn't carry such a thing with her, and ice-related sorcery wasn't her specialty. Itsuwa fished around in her pocket, took out a hand towel, and gently pressed it to Kamijou's arms. She sighed in relief—his wounds seemed to be shallow.

What about Terra of the Left...? thought Itsuwa idly as she did first aid. *And the document...Did Terra cause this disaster? This doesn't seem like the type of thing he's been doing until now...*

Had they won, or had they lost?

She couldn't even tell that much.

From a cursory glance, the Imagine Breaker's wounds were shallow. For now, it was best to wait until he woke up and have him explain the situation. And if need be, chase down Terra, even this very moment.

"..."

She hadn't been involved in the fight with Terra the whole way through. She'd passed out in the middle, pushing the rest onto this amateur of a boy.

Itsuwa quietly clenched her teeth at her powerlessness. *I have to do something...*

But crisis situations never give people the time.

"Tsk. This is turning out to be a big pain in the ass."

Suddenly, she heard a voice that made tension shoot through her body.

Its quality itself was ominous, but what surprised her most was the direction it came from.

Readying her spear, eyes wide in disbelief, she turned to look.

Ahead of her.

To the passage turned into goopy molten lava from high heat.

That was the direction she thought she'd heard the voice from.

She couldn't make out the person's features because of the shroud of steam. But she could tell just from the sight of his silhouette that he was standing there in a completely natural pose.

Despite being stopped in the middle of the thousand-degree lava.

...In the midst of all the steam, which must have been over a hundred degrees by itself.

"Guess you gotta think about stuff being *too* strong, eh? 'Sides, why'd you point those earth-cutting blades at a person? Would've been more helpful to check for a corpse. Well, the riots calmed right down around the time you did the cutting, so at least our minimum objective is complete now..."

The person wasn't paying any attention to her.

He wasn't even looking at her.

His words were not for Itsuwa. He was probably using a radio or cell phone, talking to someone far away.

And Itsuwa thought that was fine.

She could feel a strange sweat bursting from the hands on her spear.

She didn't know the reason. But the person standing in the middle of that molten rock was extraordinary. How she could fight against him, what miracle would let her win—he was more than a little bit past that stage. If she had to compare, it felt only like swinging a delicate spear at a giant ball of iron.

He spoke.

Without even seeing the blade-holding Itsuwa.

"Sure, I'll inspect the place for a corpse and everything, but if I don't find anything in ten minutes, I'm coming back. Later, once things cool off here, you guys can do your searching for loose hairs and bloodstains and all that DNA analysis or whatever. Eh? Recover the disabled powered suit? I ain't here to do chores. Make your guys do it. There's gotta be a group or agency or something here in France that's on Academy City's side."

That was where the conversation ended.

Was his talk with the distant person over?

"..."

Like an herbivore hidden in the foliage to wait out a savage beast, Itsuwa held her breath.

Her opponent didn't give one look to her.

Immeasurable.

Itsuwa ignored her trembling hands as they gripped her spear

and then turned her back to the figure. He seemed to want to head deeper into the Papal Palace; she watched him disappear farther down the trail of molten rock.

She didn't follow him.

She couldn't even speak to him.

Even after the unknown figure vanished, Itsuwa was too nervous to move for a while.

In an interrogation room in the Tower of London, Stiyl Magnus and Agnes Sanctis were listening to what Lidvia Lorenzetti had to say. Biagio Busoni, also present, seemed intent on acting uncooperatively throughout and never opened his mouth to say anything.

"In Crossism, God never appeared after the Son of God's death," said Lidvia, her voice echoing through the confined interrogation room. "In exchange, his angels, acting as his hands and feet, appear before humans with considerable frequency. Still, added to the story of a great war between angels and demons, a certain theologian felt the need to categorize them into nine groups, but they may simply be great in number."

"What's that have to do with this?" prompted Stiyl.

Lidvia continued, without so much as a nod. "What I mean is that God's Right Seat is a pragmatic organization. Does a god who doesn't appear before man truly exist? Might not God be taking the form of angels to secretly contact humans? Those who think that, chasing the shadow of whatever it is pretending to be the angels, are God's Right Seat."

In other legends besides Crossist ones, it was not unusual to hear of gods changing into something else and coming to earth… whether that thing was equal to humans or purposely below them.

Those are the ideas mixed in here? wondered Stiyl, filing it away in a corner of his mind. "…How does that connect to the name 'God's Right Seat'? I believe you mentioned it being their ultimate objective at the same time as their organization's name."

"Man cannot become God." Instead of answering directly, Lidvia continued her own story. "There are plenty of supposed methods for doing so, but we have received no reports of one working. However, one step lower—angels, in other words—and we do have reports of certain disciplines, such as alchemy, demonstrating such an evolution…These too, of course, are incredibly rare, however.

"In other words," she declared, "they're looking for a way to become an angel after erasing the original sin binding them as human. Not just any mere angel, mind you. That which borrows the form of angels and manifests upon the earth—using the true 'god' angel, which pretends to be an angel as a sample."

The hubris to, despite acknowledging God's power, not let it end there and attempt to wrest that power from him.

To add to that, there was no foundation for the story of God coming to earth disguised as an angel in the first place.

Stiyl's lips twisted into a smile. "…What a splendid heretical cult."

"At the moment, they're targeting the angel Michael, born as the other half of the pair to Lucifer, who was strongest amongst all angels." Lidvia's voice was level. "For Lucifer is the only angel permitted to sit at the right hand of God. And Michael, who defeated Lucifer to become the leader of all the angels, was on Lucifer's level or higher—that is what God's Right Seat believes."

The right side.

In Crossism, "the right" referred to equality. One of the first Crossist martyrs, the disciple Stephen, had used the word *right* to refer to the one God as an expression of honor in the Son of God, expressing that the Son of God was an "equivalent" existence to God.

He had used the term *right* for the Son of God because of the idea of the Holy Trinity, to say that God and the Son of God were to be honored equally.

But what about the angels?

Why could Lucifer sit at "the right," and Michael still have enough power to defeat the one sitting there? By nature, the Christian God was a unique existence. If God stood at the world's summit, then he wouldn't let anyone sit at his "equal" right. To say nothing of the difficulty of believing a mere angel being granted that right, when they were created as tools and servants of him.

Despite that, an angel, supposedly lower in rank, had been there and that held special importance—or so they seemed to think.

"Their aim is to sit at the right seat of God. And once they attain that position, they can transform from angels to something more... or so they seem to believe."

And the name of that something was—

"La persona superiore a Dio..."

Hearing those flowing words caused Stiyl and Agnes to knit their eyebrows.

In other words...

"...the one who is above God, or *kami-jou*, as they call it."

Footsteps echoed through St. Peter's Basilica in the Vatican.

The pace was thoroughly constant. Slow and measured. Its rhythm had a looseness, a calmness that showed the mental state of its owner.

Then those footsteps abruptly stopped.

A figure had appeared in front of their owner.

"Terra."

"Acqua, eh...?" said the owner—Terra of the Left—shortly, turning a glare on Acqua of the Back, who had appeared before him. It sounded like Terra had been thinking to himself and found it bothersome to interrupt that for a conversation.

The supersonic bombers that had attacked Terra in the Papal Palace had been immensely strong, but they were all one type of the same attack to him, so he could block them all with his prioritization. More dreadful to him was several different attacks coming at the same time.

"I presume the Document of Constantine has been lost."

"Yes," Terra admitted easily. "They used the usual Imagine Breaker, so recovery would be difficult."

"You nevertheless seem to be in quite a good mood."

"Ha-ha," laughed Terra with a thin smile. "Acqua, you've been having some talks of your own, haven't you?

"I hear the Russian Catholic Church has officially decided to ally with us."

Acqua fell silent for a moment.

Eventually, he opened his mouth. "We are Roman Orthodox followers. Clinging to the cooperation of other denominations isn't normally praiseworthy."

"Heh-heh. We're only using them, that's all. And I'm sure they think the same way."

The relaxation hadn't gone from Terra's face.

He wasn't broken yet.

"During the document incident, Academy City and the English Puritan Church were acting in concert behind the scenes," announced Terra. "Of course, I'm sure neither would be willing to admit it."

"But more importantly is how the Russian Church feels now that they know..."

"Academy City and the English Puritans have already built a kind of channel between them. If the Russian Catholics offered cooperation as newcomers, they would not necessarily sip that sweet honey. They seek the winner's profits in this little war, and so the science side winning would not be agreeable for them...Maybe that's how they're feeling."

Currently, Academy City and the Vatican were balanced in terms of combat power.

That was why the actions of third parties, such as the Puritans and the Russian Catholicism, became important.

If at all possible, it was desirable to invite those two as collaborators on the "sorcery side." But the English Church had already set up a connection with Academy City.

And as one could see from the incidents with the *Book of the Law,*

Orsola, the Daihasei Festival, and the Croce di Pietro, there was a deep divide sitting between the camps of the Roman and English churches.

Therefore, they would purposely give up on the English Puritans. To avoid the worst case—both the English and Russian churches allying with the science side—they had to draw the Russian Catholics' attention to them at all costs.

That was what the Document of Constantine was for.

Losing the Soul Arm was unfortunate, but it meant they'd accomplished the goal they had at the outset.

"Anyway, this means we have the Roman and Russian churches on one side, and Academy City and the English Puritans on the other. Still, Academy City and the English Church are from different worlds, so I'm sure fractures will appear between them. Now that we have Russia's support, we have a firm foothold with which to invade Japan. We have the knife to their necks…We may want to consult with Fiamma of the Right and decide our own actions henceforth. I'd wanted to look into Academy City's response patterns and the Imagine Breaker a little more, but I suppose I've done enough."

"I see. But before you do that, I have something to say to you."

Acqua's voice was severe.

And so Terra replied lightly, "What is it?"

"Oh, nothing difficult. I received a report you were *making use of* children and tourists in the Roman suburbs to do targeting alignments for that special spell of yours nobody else can use, the Light's Execution. Is that true?"

"Yes, it is," confirmed Terra surprisingly easily.

But…

"Is that worth any particular mention, though?"

Terra of the Left finished with that.

Acqua's eyes narrowed. "…I recall you were acting to grant equal salvation to all humanity. Were you not acting out of a desire to know if when man was led to the holy land by his faith, whether their factional problems would continue amongst them?"

"Yes, yes," answered Terra, making a face that said it was a stupid question. "I do certainly want to grant salvation to all humanity equally, but heretics aren't human in the first place. Acqua, did you check over the documents carefully? I was scrupulous in determining that my targets were not of Roman Orthodoxy before using them as 'targets' to adjust the aim."

"..."

"Ah, are you worried about the heinous criminals they couldn't execute coming here via Spain? Allow me to make a report—I will not lay a hand on them. They are believers in the Roman Orthodox Crossist tradition and objects of my salvation. My subordinates have a habit of bringing out criminals as soon as I mention needing people, but that will not do. If I am to exhaust people as targets, they must not be Roman Orthodox believers."

This was "equality" according to Terra.

He spoke of saving all humanity, but his definition of "human" was incredibly narrow from the start. He considered it reasonable to treat those who didn't fit his conditions to be human as mere livestock. Such were the ideas pervading this clergyman's very foundations.

When Acqua of the Back remained silent, Terra continued, sounding bothered. "They will visit purgatory and wash the sins clinging to their souls, thereby gaining a path to the holy land. Their first step is to surrender their lives to we of the clergy. Those who cannot do even that haven't the right to fall to purgatory—they can only suffer for eternity in hell."

"...I see," answered Acqua shortly. "You mean to say you've been doing regular maintenance on that spell ever since you acquired it."

"Yes, now please move out of the way, Acqua. I have a very big pile of things on my plate. I must consider our next attack against the science side, as well as improve on various aspects of my prioritization spell, as I seem to have found a...habit, let's say. And I think that will require slight targeting modifications."

"Actually, there's one thing you need to do before that."

The word *what?* almost made it out of Terra's mouth.

Because with a tremendous roar...

Terra of the Left's body, this time for sure, shattered into pieces.

What Acqua of the Back had just done was extremely simple.

He had broken off one of the pillars supporting St. Peter's ceiling, swung it around with one hand, and beaten it into Terra's body. That was all he did, and yet its overwhelming might and speed made it look like a raging windstorm.

Terra of the Left's favored prioritization spell—Light's Execution.

A wondrous spell to have staved off even Academy City's large-scale supersonic bombing, but Acqua of the Back wouldn't let him use it at all.

Drip. Drip.

The sound was from Terra of the Left, who had lost most of his body, left only with his upper chest, head, and right arm.

"Oh...ah...?"

Terra looked up at him, his face mystified as to what had happened. He seemed to be trying to close the wounds using Light's Execution, but his mind appeared to fail at constructing the spell, as nothing happened.

Acqua of the Back looked down at him, watching, eyes full of contempt. Terra's mind was still alive. But Terra wasn't responsible for his current condition. Acqua had killed him so quickly that his physical life reactions were still present.

"Hu...ha..."

He heard a noise he couldn't distinguish between a voice or a breath.

Acqua frowned. He'd just smashed Terra to pieces, but he wasn't afraid of death. There was calm on his face.

"...Is there something wrong, Terra of the Left?" asked Acqua, realizing the answer before he heard it.

The holy land.

For Terra, death was no more than part of the road to salvation. Even if he died here, if God chose him during the Last Judgment and welcomed him into the holy land, Terra would be saved.

He's quite a man in his own right. Did he still plan on playing the devout lamb, always upholding Vatican teachings, even after all this?

Acqua sighed. "Just to inform you—there is no possible way God will choose *you*. To think you still wouldn't understand that at this stage...You think you have anywhere to go but hell?"

Upon seeing Acqua's face filled with scorn, Terra's calmness disappeared.

Now there was anger.

But Acqua didn't bother to mention it and said the next words in an extremely businesslike tone.

"God knows all. For details, ask him yourself during the Last Judgment."

His life signs vanished as a hunk of meat losing its freshness, and Acqua looked away from Terra, now truly and genuinely no more than a stain on the floor.

When he did, a new figure appeared from behind one of the pillars in the colonnade.

An old man, bent at the waist—the pope of Rome.

He gazed between the human flesh lying nearby and the pillar Acqua had put on the floor. "This is St. Peter's Basilica. I would appreciate it if you didn't destroy things on a whim."

"I apologize," said Acqua, lowering his head to the criticism. "I should have refrained from fighting here, considering its historical and academic importance. I'm sorry for damaging a prominent building."

"...This is also the Roman Orthodox Church's most important bastion, though. I would have suspicions about its defensive capabilities if something so slight were to destroy it."

"Hmm." Acqua thought for a moment. Eventually, he said, "That issue applies not only to St. Peter's Basilica but to everything. God's

Right Seat, for example. However excellent the organization, however talented the people gathered to it, a single rampage leads to thorough destruction. Like Terra, this time."

"…"

"Your aim is God's Right Seat, and you believe you can directly grant salvation to even more followers by becoming superior to God. Your viewpoint is valuable, but that is not enough."

Acqua gazed straight into the pope's eyes.

"For God's Right Seat to maintain its functions, it must have someone to keep watch over it and lead it from outside. And I believe you are the most suited for that role."

Upon hearing those words, the old man smiled thinly. "When I heard of God's Right Seat, though, it made me happy—no other method would be simpler to lead the faithful…," he said. "But God does not desire simple salvation. Our Father, who watches over us, seems to have quite a taste for trials."

Acqua nodded at the pope's assertion.

"What will your next action be?"

"Vento can't act. And I purged Terra. There is only one thing left."

"You intend to attack Japan through Russia, as Terra said?"

"This incident taught me something. As expected, civilians should not stand on the battlefield. Only soldiers need to cross blades with one another."

That was a silent implication that he would be the one to make the next debut.

Acqua of the Back.

Thinking back upon his trait, the pope muttered, "…So it will be you—both a member of God's Right Seat and one possessed of the qualities of a saint."

Mikoto Misaka was frozen in place, cell phone in hand.

After hearing the static-filled words from the other end of the speaker, she could no longer move. A cold sweat broke out all over her body.

Kamijou had no way of knowing—but even with his phone's LCD broken and its fold-up joint twisted out of place, it wasn't as though it had lost its calling capabilities. In other words, the conversation between Kamijou and Terra in the Papal Palace had made its way over the phone and into Mikoto's ear.

She didn't understand most of their exchange. Actually, even if she had, she would have forgotten most of it.

Only one thing was tightening around her heart now.

"…"

She tried to say it, but realized her voice wasn't working.

She moved her trembling hands, managing to turn off her cell phone's power, and stared for a while at the disconnected phone. She wanted to stay still until the quaking stopped, but no matter how long she waited, it showed no signs of doing so.

Still, she was coming out of her shock a little at a time, and soon, she moved her lips. She didn't intend for it, but she could hear her own voice from her mouth, unnaturally hoarse.

She gave a soft mutter.

"…For…got…?"

After saying it aloud, she thought about what that meant again. Amnesia?

AFTERWORD

For those of you who have been getting these books one volume at a time, it's good to see you again.

For those of you who bought all of them at once, it's a pleasure to meet you.

I'm Kazuma Kamachi.

Volume 14 had a lot of things start to happen. I decided to bring out all the problems the series hasn't touched on very much—the ones I saved for later.

The overarching theme is that of the "group." As for the occult keyword, I suppose it's the "Last Judgment." Several things, some of course related to the Last Judgment directly but others indirectly, are incorporated into this (the more easily understood ones include original sin and Mass).

…Actually, I feel like all the Crossist bits, wherever you look, are related to the Last Judgment, but I guess the point is that this volume was more aware of it than usual.

If I had to pick one, the story ended up being magic side-ish, but with the heaps of new Academy City weapons showing up, I believe I've set it up to grant those of you on the science side some peace of mind.

Thank you to my illustrator, Mr. Haimura, and my editor, Mr. Miki. This was a pretty jumbled-up story, but seriously, thank you so much for sticking with me. I'd like to thank Mr. Jun'ichi Manaka this time as well. His lecture on military topics, such as how stealth fighters work, was incredibly useful. I'd also like to thank Ms. Yuuko Fukushima. Her supervision on the Italian language was a huge help.

And to all my readers. Including the short story volume, this series has reached its fifteenth book. Me coming this far was all thanks to you. I look forward to your continued support.

Now then, as you close this page now,
and as I pray you will open the first page next time,
here now, I lay down my pen.

Now, what of the difference between these two *kami-jou*—"superior to God" and "the cleansing of God"…?

Kazuma Kamachi

Congratulations on Volume 14's release!

Hello, nice to meet you.

My name is Kogino.

I currently have the pleasure

of working on the first volume

of Index for the magazine

Shounen Gangan.

I want to express the charm

of Kamachi-sensei's

characters as much as I can...

I train every day. It's a high wall...

I look forward to your support m(_ _)m

2007.10.

Chuya Kogino

Nice to meet you!

I'm Motoi Fuyukawa, the one fortunate enough to be working on the *Index* side story *A Certain Scientific Railgun* in a magazine called *Dengeki Daioh*.

The manga depicts things behind the scenes during the events of the original novels, with the young lady Mikoto Misaka, aka "Biri Biri," as the central figure.

I'm still inexperienced in every field possible, but please support me, the novels, and the *Gangan* adaptation!

冬川 基

Motoi Fuyukawa